UNDER AN ORANGE SUN

SOME DAYS ARE BLUE

IRVING BELATECHE

Laurel Canyon Press

Laurel Canyon Press, November 2011

Library of Congress Control Number: 2011916887

ISBN 978-0-9840265-0-0

Cover Design by Glendon S. Haddix
Cover Painting: "Impression, Soleil Levant" (Impression, Sunrise), Claude Monet

Printed in the United States of America

Laurel Canyon Press
Los Angeles, California

1

Sarah, my beautiful, six-year-old daughter, is dead. She's lying in front of me in a hospital bed, in a sterile hospital room. I knew she might die, but I never believed she actually would. Her eyes are closed, but she doesn't look peaceful. I want her to look peaceful. I want her to be peaceful. I want that more than anything in the world.

I want her to be happy that all her suffering is over. But she loved life so much that I can't fool myself into believing she's happy. She'd much rather be playing hide-and-seek with Emma, her best friend, checking out every nook and cranny in our house for a good place to hide. She could live with her pain because she loved life. The joy of life was greater than the pain. For Sarah, I know that was true. I saw it.

I'm already accepting that wanting her back is foolish. I'm not naïve enough to believe that she'll come back. That harsh reality has already sunk in. Cold, mean, and final.

And I also don't believe her spirit has moved on. I don't believe her spirit is glad to be free of its earthly bonds. I don't believe that Sarah has found joy somewhere else. And I can't fool myself into believing that some good is going to come out of this and I know I won't ever be able to.

From this day forward, I know that everything will be different. I'm not sure if my life is over, but I know I'll never be happy again. I can feel it. I've always been an optimist. I've always believed that things eventually swing back my way no matter how bad they get. I don't believe that anymore.

Everything I believe in has been obliterated. Sarah, my beautiful daughter, full of life, is dead. The leukemia killed her. My optimism, my good thoughts, my prayers, couldn't stop the leukemia. State-of-the-art medicine couldn't stop it. There was no miracle.

Now what?

2

I want to protect my son. He's in the room, and he's watched his twin sister die. Will he ever recover? He's crying. So are my wife and I.

My wife wanted my son here. She'd backed it up with professional opinions and she was sure in her soul that this was the right thing to do. I'd been conflicted about it. I'd been leaning toward not having him here. But when the time came, and it came swiftly at the end, there was no time for debate. My wife's certainty in her belief was way more powerful than my wavering.

But now I'm thinking that this is the worst thing I've ever done. Why should my son have watched his twin sister die? He's way too young to face the finality of death.

We stay with Sarah for a while. It's hard to leave her. Once we leave this sterile room, she'll be alone forever. She'll never see her parents or her brother again. *I'll never see her again.*

And I'm sure that I'll never see her as a spirit. I don't believe she's gone on to live as a spirit, or as an angel, or as some other form of life. But what I don't know at that moment, what I could never fathom, is that my belief will soon change. Accepting that my child is gone forever is hard. Harder than I thought.

It's much easier to accept that everything has changed and that nothing will ever be the same. My life has just been cleaved in half, optimism to one side, sadness to the other. Optimism in the past, sadness in the future.

3

The next few days are a blur. Everything is out of kilter. I'm feeling the strongest emotions I've ever felt. They change everything around me and inside me, and not for the better. They make everything hollow and insignificant. They take the life out of life.

I also feel unlucky. Cursed. I don't know if that's peculiar to losing a child, but that's what I feel. I don't tell anyone. It's not their problem and it makes me feel selfish. I'm not the one who died. Why should I feel cursed?

When I step out of my house, the outside world is totally removed from me. People are buying their morning coffee at Starbucks and window-shopping on Ventura Boulevard. They have no idea how vicious the world is. How can they go about their mundane business when my daughter just died?

I want to stop them and tell them that this sweet, innocent life was cut down for no reason. I never consider the possibility that some of these people are hiding their own tragedies. I can't see through the thick, black cloud of death that enshrouds me.

I go into Von's to buy some bread and lettuce and I'm repelled by the other people shopping for groceries. They don't get it. They don't understand that tragedy is just around the corner, a crushing sadness waiting to spring on them.

I wait in the checkout line and overhear customers chattering. Every conversation sounds like blathering, irrelevant and trivial. Why aren't these people talking about Sarah's death?

I notice a tabloid headline above the candy rack. It doesn't mention Sarah's death, but at least it mentions death. Its headline promises an amazing account of a celebrity's near-death experience and that reminds me of something I'd once heard.

People who've gone through a near-death experience see a different world after they recover. They feel a connection to everyone around them. A connection they've never felt before. Their hearts are open and they feel compassion toward everyone.

I realize that I feel the exact opposite. My heart is open, but it's open because it's bleeding from a terrible wound. And I don't feel compassion toward everyone. I feel resentment and sadness toward everyone. I feel resentment because they're going about their business as if my tragedy means nothing. And I feel sadness because they don't realize how fragile life is. How fragile *their* lives are. Not because death might strike them at any time, but because of something much worse. Death might strike someone they love at any time.

I also remember that people who've had near-death

experiences say that their feeling of compassion toward everyone vanishes after a few weeks. I hope that my feelings of resentment and sadness vanish. I hope this feeling that I'm living in a separate world vanishes.

Then, as I reach out through the black cloud of death, to pay the cashier, I suddenly realize what this separate world actually is. It's a deadworld. I'm living in a deadworld, and I wonder if I'll ever be able to climb out of it.

But as I walk out of Von's, I realize that I don't want to climb out of it. *My deadworld connects me to Sarah.*

4

The funeral is surreal. It's a true out-of-body experience. For me, not for Sarah. I wish it were for Sarah. I wish it were Sarah's spirit floating above me in the church. Then I could believe that she lived on.

But Sarah's spirit isn't up there. *I'm* up there, floating above the memorial service, above relatives and friends, above the flowers and photos, above Sarah's collection of snow globes and stuffed kitties, gloomy substitutes for what's missing, Sarah, herself.

After the funeral, friends and relatives step up to my wife and me and offer their condolences. Some are genuinely upset at Sarah's death and I love them. Some try to say the right thing and some even know that the best thing to say is nothing. They don't know what to say and neither do I.

Evelyn, an older woman whom I know well, says the wrong thing. She says that God has a reason for everything and that some good will come out of this. That makes me angry. Not because she's blurting out a platitude, but because she believes it. She's an evangelical Christian and she believes that God has a master plan and that murdering my daughter is part of His plan.

But even though I'm angry, I do have to admit that her belief is better than mine. I believe that Sarah's death was a random tragedy that I may have accidentally caused. Evelyn's belief contains some good. Mine is nothing but bleak sadness.

At the reception, Susie, my sister-in-law and favorite relative, tosses another platitude at me. *God gives us only what we can bear.*

Like Evelyn, Susie is a Christian, but she's not fanatical. She's a Christian who believes that Christianity means helping the less fortunate. She's kind, easygoing, and thoughtful. If every Christian were like Susie, I'd have signed up a long time ago.

But in this case, she didn't help the less fortunate, me. Susie said the wrong thing. She sees the anger on my face and she immediately backtracks. She explains that my wife and I are two of the strongest people she knows and not many people could make it through a tragedy like this, but she's sure we can. That's all she meant.

I see that she feels awful and I know that she's truly a good person. She was devastated when she heard that Sarah had been diagnosed with leukemia and she did everything she could to help us during Sarah's treatments.

So I tell her that I understand and, since she and I have had many honest conversations in the past, I also tell her exactly what I don't like about the religious platitudes that people are lobbing at me. It's the God part. God and I are on bad terms right now. I just can't believe that, if there is a God, He plans to murder your daughter.

Susie is understanding. She doesn't mind discussing her faith in such negative terms and we end up comparing religious platitudes. Everything from "Sarah's in a better place" to "God needed her more than we did." In the end, fanatical Evelyn's platitude fairs better than most. Susie explains the platitude in a way that almost makes sense.

God's master plan is like a tapestry that He's been weaving since time began. He looks down at the tapestry from above, and from His point of view, it's beautiful and perfect. But we look at the tapestry from below and we see the underside. We see the ugly knots and the loose threads that He's tied off and the tapestry looks like a big, hideous mess.

Jack, my father—in-law, doesn't say anything to me at the funeral or at the reception, or over the next few days. I wonder if he's going to acknowledge Sarah's death at all. Not that it would be out of character for him if he didn't. He's a big bear of a man, a blue-collar guy with a great temperament. He never passes judgment and he takes life as it comes, the good with the bad. Jack doesn't talk much under any circumstances.

A few days after the funeral, he and my mother-in-law are ready to head back east. They're in our foyer, with their bags in the rental car outside, and we're exchanging goodbyes. By now, I've accepted that Jack isn't going to say anything to me about Sarah. Then, just before he steps out of the house, he grabs me and hugs me hard and says, "There'll be better days ahead."

He doesn't let go of me. It's an all-encompassing hug, like he's transferring some comfort and wisdom directly to me. Then he suddenly lets go and heads out.

As he and my mother-in-law climb into their rental car, I think, of all the condolences I've heard, that's the oddest one. Sure, it's a platitude, but when he'd said it, it hadn't sound like one. It hadn't sounded phony either. It had just sounded odd.

I watch Jack drive off and I'm stumped. Why didn't this platitude sound like a cliché? It was a classic cliché, one of the all-time greats. And why didn't it sound phony? *There'll be better days ahead.* It should've sounded phony.

At that moment, I had no answers to my questions. But I do now. Amidst all the platitudes and clichés that I'd heard, this one had been true. *There'll be better days ahead.* It was the unvarnished, unadorned truth, delivered by a man who'd seen a lot of life.

Jack hadn't said, you'll see *good* days ahead. He'd said you'll see *better* days ahead. He had told me the truth before I was ready to hear it and understand it. He'd tried to break through the black cloud of death that enshrouded me. He'd tried to deliver a piece of wisdom into my deadworld.

Any day when my daughter doesn't die is better than the day she did die. Even if it's not a good day, it has to be a better day.

5

The rest of our relatives head back home. Our friends go back to their lives. And after a couple more weeks of limbo, my wife, my son, and I head back out into the world.

Rachel, my wife, has to find a completely new life. She quit her job four years ago to take care of Sarah, full-time, and now, Sarah, the center of her every waking moment, is gone.

Rachel joins a grief group and she vows to spend as much time as possible with Jake, our son. She wants to make up for abandoning him for four years. In no way did she abandon him, but that's how she feels. Jake played second fiddle to Sarah because Sarah needed her mom more than he did. But he played second fiddle with dignity and courage. At times, with more dignity and courage than I did.

Rachel wants me to go with her to the grief group, but I can't. Some vestige of my former self has stayed intact. I believe that I can overcome this grief by myself. The only person who can change me is me.

That belief is ingrained in me.

Before the grand cleaving of my life, I believed that a careful and precise marshalling of my thoughts could change anything. Both internally and externally. I believed that my thoughts were like an army ready to do my bidding. Even though I was a hardcore rationalist, I'd seen evidence that I could change both my internal and external realities by changing my thoughts, and by implementing certain Principles.

But right now, I'm facing the harsh truth that I wasn't able to change the most important reality in my life. I wasn't able to prevent Sarah's death and I was fairly sure that I wasn't going to be able to bring her back. These immutable facts undercut all my previous beliefs. Either I could change everything or I could change nothing. I have to resolve this dilemma. It's a standoff.

The outside world comments on my and Rachel's fortitude and continues to give us its condolences. We cry. A lot. Eventually the outside world forgets that we've suffered a great tragedy and moves on. We don't.

Rachel and I talk about our grief with each other, but we have a fundamental disagreement that colors every conversation. She believes there wasn't anything we could've done to save Sarah. I believe there was something we could've done, but, instead, we did the wrong thing.

I believe we could've saved Sarah by making different medical choices, and I spend time rehashing each of those choices. This drives Rachel crazy. She believes Sarah was one of the fifteen percent of childhood leukemia victims who don't make it. I believe Sarah should've been one of the eighty-five percent who *do* make it.

But we never talk about this for too long because, not only does this conversation drive Rachel crazy, it also makes her think that I blame her for Sarah's death. I don't. I blame myself. But we never get to that part. Instead, we end up arguing or consoling each other.

Rachel is looking for answers, but unlike me, who hasn't come up with a plan, she's taking the more traditional route. In addition to her grief group, she's reading books about coping with the loss of a child and she's talking to her friends.

I try to read some of those books, but I give up. I don't find comfort in them and I don't find answers. And I *don't* talk to my friends about Sarah. I get the sense that my friends don't want to talk about her. They don't want to be reminded that crushing sadness is waiting for us just around the corner. They don't want to dwell on the harsh reality that Sarah is dead and gone forever. I don't blame them. I don't really want to dwell on it either.

I go back to work.

6

For over a decade and half, I've made my living as a screenwriter. During all that time, I've never had a problem focusing on my writing. Now I do. It's hard. Really hard.

I'm used to spending hours and hours in my cave writing an unending stream of stories. I call my office my "cave" because it sequesters me from all the distractions of the outside world. I can live in my imagination for weeks and write uninterrupted by life.

During Sarah's illness, I wrote in my cave and I enjoyed writing as much as I ever did. And when I say "enjoy," I don't mean "enjoy" as if writing is different from any other profession. A writer has days when he or she enjoys writing and gets lost in the process. But a writer has just as many days when writing is a slog. A long, painful, and torturous slog.

Thomas Mann once said, "A writer is someone for whom writing is more difficult than it is for other people." I couldn't agree with him more. He was talking about those slog days. A writer is someone who makes it through those slog days.

I'm always suspicious of writers who "love" to write. I suspect that they don't write that much. A writer is someone who loves writing some of the time and powers through it the rest of the time. A writer is someone who's *driven* to write and not someone who "loves" to write.

I was still driven to write during Sarah's long battle with leukemia, so I can't figure out why my writing is harder now than it was during the darkest days of her illness. It has something to do with that "drive." The drive that encompasses the love of writing and the compulsion to write. The drive that powers a writer through his or her slog days.

At first, I don't say anything about this to Rachel. Over the last four years, my income as a screenwriter, plus the health insurance that came with it, was critical to our lives and to Sarah's survival. We're still counting on that income and we're still reeling from our loss, so I'm not going to add some angst about my writing, what may just be the longest slog in the world, to her problems.

She's trying hard to work through her loss. She's doing all the right things and it's still brutally tough. She's the bravest person I know and if only one of us is going to make it out of the deadworld, I want it to be her. I'm not going to pile on and ruin her chances. I'm not going to be the anchor that keeps her tied down to the deadworld.

But one night, I return home from my cave and Rachel asks me how my writing is going, and it's clear she's not just making conversation. She's looking right at me and she's sincere.

I don't lie. I tell her I'm having a hard time getting back to work.

She tells me to take more time off, don't push yourself so hard. Tears well up in her eyes and I can tell she wants me to talk about Sarah. She thinks that might help my writing. But I don't want to talk about Sarah. So I don't.

7

I can't take time off. I can't stop writing. My life is empty enough without Sarah. So rather than take time off, I decide that I need to figure out why my writing has become harder.

I jump to the obvious answer first. The answer that Rachel wanted to talk about last night. Sarah is gone. Her death, so final and sad, has extinguished that mysterious fire which fuels my drive to write.

Then, from this answer, I jump to something that isn't quite so obvious. *I need a sign.* I need a sign from Sarah. I need her to tell me she's okay. If she tells me she's okay, she'll rekindle that mysterious fire. If she tells me she's okay, I can write again.

I realize this is crazy, but I want that sign.

Luckily I live in Los Angeles so it isn't hard for me to find people who don't think this is crazy. In L.A., normal people hold all kinds of irrational beliefs. And they're confident in those beliefs.

I also know that talking to these people about this sign won't depress them. A sign from Sarah implies that the harsh reality of death isn't so harsh. A sign means that she's still alive somewhere.

I mention my search to a few people whom I know are into New Age thinking. They're happy when I bring it up and some even confess that they had wanted to bring it up themselves. But they'd thought I was way too conservative and I'd find it disrespectful.

Now that they know I'm open to something this crazy, they all make the same suggestion. Contact a medium, and they give me the names of mediums who can speak to the dead. I research them and find that a few have high-profile clients. I'm even tempted to see one of them, but I discover that my former self, the one on the other side of the grand divide that cleaves my life, continues to wield great influence. I have a hard time accepting that some random person will be able to contact my dead daughter.

My wife is sad, my son is confused, and there's an emptiness in our house that I feel every time I step inside it. If Sarah's spirit were around, I wouldn't feel that emptiness. If Sarah's spirit were around, it would come to me and say something. Sarah would give me a sign herself. She wouldn't need to speak through a medium.

I mention my empty house to one of the people who wants me to talk to a medium and she has an explanation. She tells me that after a person dies, his or her spirit doesn't stick around for too long. It moves on. She says I don't feel Sarah's spirit because it's in the process of moving on. She may have already moved on. She tells me the longer I wait to contact

Sarah's spirit, the harder it'll be. Sarah is moving farther and farther away.

I'm shocked. Not because this is a crazy response to what I'm feeling, but because it makes perfect sense. I don't know if I believe in a spirit world but, if I were a spirit, and could go anywhere in the universe, I know I'd be out there exploring. Why would I stick around the family that I died in? They're weighed down by grief and it's too much sadness to bear. Especially when I can now go anywhere in the universe.

This still doesn't drive me to a medium yet, but I wonder if Sarah is slipping farther away and that makes me sadder than I was.

8

Susie, my sister-in-law, visits and, one night, she and Rachel talk for a long while about Sarah. I don't participate and it's noticeable. I can see that Susie is upset. She came here to help, but how can she help if I don't want to talk about the only thing that matters.

After Rachel and Jake go to bed, I go back into the kitchen and I find Susie sitting at the kitchen table. She's looking through a photo album of photos of Sarah. Susie is smiling a sad smile like her heart is open and she's letting Sarah in.

Even though I don't want to, and she doesn't ask me to, her open heart draws it out of me. I talk about Sarah in the only way I know how. I mention my crazy idea about a sign.

I tell her, *I want a sign.*

I'm like a baby demanding something I can't have. Susie takes my irrational demand seriously and she says that I already have a sign. She's talking about one of Sarah's poems.

Sarah wrote some beautiful poems during her short stay. Poems that seemed to spring from a well of wisdom that only she had access to. She could reach into this well and pull out a poem fully formed. She used to dictate them to Rachel and me. No rewriting necessary.

Susie reaches into the back of the photo album and pulls out a poem Sarah wrote a few weeks before she died. None of us, including Sarah, had any idea she'd be gone so soon afterward. She was doing well when she wrote the poem. That's why Susie says it's a sign.

I brace myself and I read the poem. I haven't read it in a long, long time. It's called "Goodbye, My Friend."

The river is wavy.
The boats are crowded.
The subways are packed,
The road is flooded.

My house has no roof,
The windows are cracked.
I will love you forever,
But now I must go.

I will remember in my heart,
How we skipped and jumped
And played together.
I will love you forever
But now I must go.

Tears stream down my face and I quickly wipe them away. I don't believe this is a sign. *I will love you forever, but now I must go.* She's not talking to me. It's a coincidence. That's all.

Susie gently disagrees. She says it's a beautiful and profound message from Sarah to me. Sarah is saying goodbye. She's telling me she has to go. *The boats are crowded, the subways are packed, the road is flooded.* There just isn't any room for her here anymore. And if that's not clear, what about her illness? *Her house has no roof, the windows are cracked.* She just can't stay here. The leukemia is killing her.

I stick to my guns. I refuse to accept that this is a sign. I want something supernatural. Something not of this world.

Susie says this is supernatural. Look how profound it is. Written by a six-year-old.

But I demand something clear and unambiguous.

Susie says that she can't think of anything more clear and unambiguous. It's right there in front of you: *I will love you forever, but now I must go.*

9

I start to look for a sign every day. Everywhere I go. But I don't see any and I still can't bring myself to go to a medium. So I lock onto another possibility.

For the last two years of Sarah's life, I didn't dream. I don't know if that was because I never slept for more than a few hours at a stretch or because I had a psychological block. Maybe I didn't need dreams because my life was surreal all the time. It felt like I was living in some kind of fatalistic netherworld where Sarah's every joy was infused with an impending doom.

Sarah's joy as she swam and fought the waves of the blue Pacific had a hyper real intensity to it. An otherworldly clarity that rose from my heartfelt pain. I knew how fragile her joy was. Her every joy might be her last. For me, her joy was the very definition of bittersweet.

Since Sarah's death, I've started to dream again. I didn't notice it at first, but now that I have, I decide that this is where I'll find my sign. This is how Sarah is going to talk to me. Sarah can visit me in my dreams.

Every night, I ask her to visit me. Every night, I hope to see her in a dream.

I don't.

10

I used to believe that anything was possible. That's why I picked up my entire life and moved it to Los Angeles. I wouldn't have pursued a career as a screenwriter if I didn't believe anything was possible.

I don't believe anything is possible anymore. I know for a fact that some things *aren't* possible. You can't save your daughter from dying no matter how hard you try. That's the sobering truth.

As the months pass, I begin to believe that this truth is the reason I find it hard to write. What if my success as a screenwriter is built on the belief that anything is possible? A belief that I now reject.

But connecting this truth to my writing feels totally selfish. My daughter is dead and here I am thinking about my career and myself. But I *have* to get back to work. I *have* to concentrate. I'm not even thinking about trying to be happy again. I don't mind being sad and stuck in my deadworld as long as I can write.

I continue to look everywhere for a sign, hoping that'll help. The dream still isn't working out. Sarah hasn't visited me. And I still can't bring myself to see a medium.

So while I continue to look for a sign, I come up with another way to try and get back to work. I decide to study my past.

11

For many years, my career followed an easy path. I sold pitches and screenplays and I was hired for rewrites. (A pitch is a story that a writer "pitches" to a studio and, if the studio buys it, they hire that writer to write the script.) But one day I stepped out of my cave and I realized that six months of no work had turned into a year, and that year had turned into two. I hadn't noticed. A screenwriter in Hollywood doesn't get a call telling him he's been fired. Instead, he gets less and less work and his phone slowly stops ringing.

And that's hard to notice because a working screenwriter works harder when he doesn't have a paying job than when he does. When he doesn't have a paying job, he stays in his cave longer, generating as many new projects as possible, to maximize the odds of selling one.

That drought was the first of my career and I wasn't sure what had caused it. My cave was never a place where I focused on the "business" part of "show business." My cave was for creating the "show" part. In my case, that meant the stories. But for the first time in my career, I had to think about the business part. I had to figure out how to turn my career back around.

And I did.

So that's the part of my life I'm going to study. It seems ridiculous to equate my current rough patch with that rough patch, as if my daughter's death is just another bump in the road, but I need to start somewhere.

I step into my office and I begin to search back through my notebooks, for the start of that rough patch.

I've been keeping notebooks since I graduated from college. They aren't diaries. They're more like progress reports about my career and about the projects I'm working on at the time. Some entries are detailed and some are brief.

I find the notebook that includes the day I stepped out of my cave and realized that I was an unemployed screenwriter. I see that this realization was a call to arms. I'd never been an unemployed screenwriter. I'd always been a *working* screenwriter. I landed my first screenwriting job while I was still in film school and I'd worked continuously until that rough patch.

In this notebook and the three that follow, I find my first attempt to decipher the secret of my success. It involved studying my past successes. I had drawn charts laying out how each of my projects had migrated from my cave to the marketplace.

The charts are detailed. For example, the first chart dissected one of my biggest pitch sales. It listed timeframes, from when I came up with the concept to when I completed the first version of the pitch, to tracking the pitch's different incarnations. It listed how and why I changed the pitch and it tracked the various failed attempts to sell it, all the way through to its triumphant sale.

The chart also listed who gave me notes on the pitch, who championed it, and who quickly jumped ship. It correlated each person's "level" in the business to the role they played.

"The business" is the self-important term Hollywood uses to refer to the film industry. And by people's "level," I mean Hollywood's crass ranking of everyone in the business. "A-level," "B-level," "C-level" and "D-level." But I didn't use that traditional ranking system in my notebooks. I saw everyone who worked in the business as either A-level or B-level. You were B-level if you were making a living in the business. You were A-level if you were making a living and you were in huge demand.

I probably used only two levels because it was self-serving. It made me B-level. But I told myself that I used two levels because I knew how hard it was to make a living as a screenwriter, or as an actor, or as a director, or as any other professional in Hollywood. I saw everyone in the business as equal, each having gained a foothold in a competitive industry. The only professionals that were more equal, A-level, were those that, either through luck or talent, or a combination of both, had risen to Hollywood royalty. (More on luck vs talent later.)

This chart was beautifully complex in its attempt to quantify the business part of show business. And it was followed by many, many more charts, just as complex.

I study a few of the charts and then I jump forward in the notebooks to find my conclusions. I see that I didn't find any consistent pattern. In the end, I didn't come up with any definitive rules that explained why one project sold and another didn't.

So my first attempt to uncover the secret of success had been a failure. It hadn't revealed a way out of my rough patch. And at that point in my notebooks, I find a break. I didn't remember a break, but it's here, right in front of me.

The notebooks pick up again much later and their contents are very different than the contents of my previous notebooks. The new notebooks reflect what happened during that break. They're centered around specific Principles. *Principles that reveal the secret of success.*

Deep down, I know what I did during that break and what led to those Principles, but I'm too embarrassed to think about it. It was something that I did without telling anyone.

12

I put the notebooks away and I start to write. But that doesn't last long. I find myself debating whether to investigate what I did during that break and this drives me out of my office and into the surrounding neighborhood.

I walk by large homes on large lots. These aren't gaudy McMansions. My office is in a guesthouse in Toluca Lake, a wealthy neighborhood in the San Fernando Valley. The neighborhood is speckled with a variety of traditional Southern California houses. Spanish colonials, Mediterraneans, Cape Cods and Tudors.

The houses are spectacular in an elegant, old-school way, like old-fashioned movie stars. Refined, stylish, and graceful. Toluca Lake isn't like the wealthy neighborhoods in Beverly Hills, where garish houses boast extravagant opulence. Those houses repel life. These houses attract it.

My walk is refreshing, but it doesn't settle the debate. Should I investigate what I did during that break or not?

Before I step back into my office, I stop to look at the garden outside my door. My landlord plants new flowers in this garden every few months so it's always drenched in vibrant color. An ocean of yellow, or blue, or orange-red. I'm not someone who stops and smells the roses, but this garden is the exception.

A stone statue of the Virgin Mary stands in the middle of the garden. During Sarah's illness, I would stand in front of Mary and pray. I prayed that she'd intercede with God to save my innocent daughter. I wasn't convinced that God existed or, that if He did, He'd involve himself with my life, but I prayed anyway.

I'm not praying now. I'm just staring at the garden, drenched in purple flowers, and I'm hoping for a sign. I'm hoping for a miracle, a vision, a revelation. Maybe the Virgin Mary will deliver this time. Maybe magic will happen right here in this garden.

And it does.

But it's not magic, itself, that happens. It's a memory *about* magic. I'm transported back to the first thing I did during the break in my notebooks.

After the complex charts failed to reveal the secret of my success, I looked for another way out of my rough patch. And what I did next is even more embarrassing than what I ended up doing. I tried the easy way out. The easiest way possible. I tried magic.

And more specifically, witchcraft. But when I say "witchcraft," I don't mean worshipping Satan. I mean spells, incantations, and potions. I mean witchcraft as it came down to us through Pagan traditions and beliefs. Before Christian authorities branded those traditions and beliefs as heretical and evil.

Once again, living in L.A. meant that pursuing magic wasn't so crazy. There were witch supply shops all over town and there were people who claimed that witchcraft and pagan rituals had turned their lives around.

I did a little due diligence before diving in. I spoke with those who claimed that these supernatural methods worked. But I didn't go as far as joining them when they practiced what they preached. Instead, I tried to find accomplished men or women who credited pagan rituals for their success. Unfortunately, I couldn't find any contemporary examples. But all was not lost.

I justified the lack of contemporary examples by convincing myself that no successful person would ever admit to believing in this stuff even if it worked. And I did dig up shaky evidence, the kind of evidence that's all over the Internet, that a few of the all-time greats, Benjamin Franklin, Thomas Jefferson, Leonardo DaVinci, and other giants from that esteemed pantheon, believed in certain pagan traditions. Their possible belief was all the validation I needed.

I lit candles, recited incantations, and performed rituals. I followed the instructions to a tee. But in the end, none of it worked. Too bad. I wanted it to work. It would've been the easy way out of my rough patch. Maybe I didn't give it enough time or maybe I didn't perform the rituals correctly, but for whatever reason, it didn't work. I moved on from witchcraft.

Before I step away from the Virgin Mary and the purple flowers that surround her, I make a connection. Is waiting for a sign from Sarah like counting on witchcraft? Am I waiting for magic? Am I looking for the easy way out of my deadworld?

13

I enter my office and I open my notebooks. The ones that started up again after that long break. I stare at the Principles inside them. I know exactly where these Principles came from and, embarrassed or not, I know that they worked. I see this in these same notebooks. The climb out of my past rough patch started as soon as I began implementing the Principles.

The Principles were distilled from a unique brand of American literature and thought. From a dirty stepchild of the Arts and Letters. From a dime store version of psychology. They came from "self-help" books. From these books, what many would call "lowbrow" books, I distilled the Principles of success.

I hadn't been able to find a pattern to my own success, so I'd decided to study success in general. This wasn't a search for happiness or spiritual enlightenment. This was a down-and-dirty search for the keys to success. I didn't even question what success meant.

I threw myself into the search by reading books,

which dealt directly with the topic. I read everything from Napoleon Hill's "Think and Grow Rich" to Maxwell Maltz's "Psycho-Cybernetics" and Tony Robbins' "Unlimited Power."

But I soon gravitated toward the early pioneers of the American self-help movement. The works of Thomas Troward, Wallace D. Wattles, James Allen, and their brethren. I don't know if I preferred these original sources because of my training as an English major or because they gave me more insights than the modern gurus. But the works of the early pioneers were imbued with an earnestness of discovery, a clarity of purpose, and a humility that I found appealing.

The modern gurus espoused many of the same principles, but I found something phony about their takes. Their books contained too much cheerleading, too much self-aggrandizement, and too many anecdotes.

Some of the self-help pioneers backed up their conclusions with the wisdom of Western civilization's greatest philosophers, so I went back to verify those claims. I read Plato's "Republic," Descartes' "Discourse of Method," Kant's "Critique of Pure Reason," and many of the other classic philosophy texts. Reading these works wasn't as daunting a task as it might seem. I'd studied the Western canon in college, so I'd already read them all.

My college believed that the Western canon provided guidance on how to live one's life. But I didn't find that guidance in college and I didn't find it this time around either. In college, I was too young to understand the question, and this time, I wasn't looking for an answer to that question. I was looking for the keys to success. I was looking for concrete "how-to" steps and it was the American self-help pioneers who were the kings of "how-to's." I didn't get any answers from Plato, Descartes, or Kant.

I also veered into reading some of the great works of Eastern philosophy and religion. I read "The Analects," the "Toa-de-ching," the "Bhagavad-Gita," and other well-known Eastern texts. That, in turn, led me to read New Age gurus like Deepak Chopra and Eckhart Tolle. I could've learned much from an Eastern definition of success, but I wasn't looking for that. I was looking for those down-and-dirty "how-to" steps.

After a long period of research, I finally stopped. Just as I knew when it was time to stop researching and start writing, I knew it was time to stop studying success and start implementing the Principles. The Principles that I'd distilled from my research.

14

For the next two days, I focus back on my writing and I don't think about my journey through the lowbrow literature of success. I leave it in the past, on the other side of the great divide, and I write haltingly and without much enthusiasm. The slog continues.

But on the fourth day, I'm thinking again about my original plan. To examine how I'd climbed out of my past rough patch. I'm thinking about the Principles. *And* I'm debating whether I should implement them. I'm desperate to find out what's wrong with my writing.

But I know what's wrong. Sarah is gone and she's never coming back. Not even in a dream. So why should I implement the Principles? *Because I have to get my career back on track.*

If I can accept that that's the only thing I expect from the Principles, they might work again. I'm not asking them to bring Sarah back.

At home, Rachel and I are reading in bed and she

puts down her book and asks me once more, if I want to go to the grief group with her. But my resistance has actually hardened. Not only do I still believe that I can overcome my grief by myself, but I've also come up with another justification for not going.

I believe that grief groups are the living incarnation of the aphorism, "misery loves company." If people are miserable, they want to find others who are miserable, so they can feel better. I've unilaterally decided that this is what grief groups are about, even though I have no evidence whatsoever to prove it.

I tell Rachel that I still don't want to go and she's disappointed. I feel bad for letting her down, but not bad enough to change my mind.

Then, a few minutes later, she asks if she can show me this on-line grief group that she's joined. It's a forum for parents who've lost their children to leukemia. She says that she finds it comforting and she'd like to share it with me. How can I say "no" to this? All I have to do is walk down the hallway to the computer.

We step out of our warm bedroom and head down the dark hallway.

In the family room, Rachel turns on the computer and brings up the website. Then she leaves me in the blue glow of the computer screen and I begin to read some of the entries.

I don't find them comforting. They magnify my grief and hopelessness. I take in the raw pain of these grieving parents and tears roll down my face.

Then I come across a posting where a woman writes that she and her husband are always fighting over how their daughter contracted leukemia. Though her daughter is gone and she's never coming back, this woman is still searching for the cause. She, like me, is desperate to find something or someone to blame. Even if that blame leads back to herself.

She writes that her husband thinks that there was nothing either of them could've done. He, like Rachel, believes that his daughter was one of the few kids unlucky enough to contract leukemia *and* one of the even fewer kids unlucky enough not to survive it.

I realize that this woman is writing about the great tension that colors every conversation between Rachel and me. The only difference is that, for this couple, their roles are reversed.

From day one, I thought that Sarah's leukemia was caused by something I did. Because my job is to sit in a cave and invent stories, I came up with hundreds of suspects in the heinous crime of Sarah's leukemia.

The list of suspects started with Sarah's childhood vaccines, moved on to viruses borne by people and animals, and then on to environmental carcinogens.

One easy target was my house. It took almost no effort to pin the crime on my defenseless house. Did it contain some weird mold that I wasn't able to uncover, even though I'd had the house inspected? Or was my house too close to those electric power lines at the edge of our back yard? Or was it too close to that radio tower on the adjacent hill? It was definitely too close to Laurel Canyon Boulevard, packed with cars spewing out carcinogenic exhaust.

Another suspect was an overly chlorinated pool that I'd taken Sarah to a number of times. And another suspect was a very sick relative whom I'd visited with Sarah when Sarah was just a few weeks old and susceptible to every nasty virus that came floating her way.

All the suspects had at least one bit of evidence that connected them to the crime. Evidence that I'd uncovered by exhaustive research, which is a writer's forte.

Rachel once tried to ease my fears by telling me about a conversation she'd had with one of the leading experts in leukemia research, as opposed to me, a leading expert in Internet research. He believed that studies would some day show that childhood leukemia was triggered by a prenatal virus that hadn't yet been isolated. In other words, this expert didn't believe that any of my suspects were guilty, or that I was to blame for delivering my daughter right into the hands of one of these villains. I didn't believe him and I still don't. I am to blame.

I find this woman's post comforting. Not because she blames herself like I do and not because I see a kindred spirit in her. But because I feel something more profound, something I never felt before. I finally understand the aphorism "misery loves company." It doesn't mean that people want to find others who are as miserable as they are, so they can feel better. It means that *they are not alone.*

For the first time since Sarah's death, I've found others in a deadworld. I can feel it. *I'm not alone.*

I log off the site, turn off the computer, and go back into the bedroom. Rachel asks me what I thought of the site. I tell her that it helped. She doesn't ask me how. Instead, she hugs me tightly and I hug her back. Neither of us says a word.

She's not alone and neither am I.

15

The next day, I arrive at my office and, before I step inside, I look at the garden. I think about Sarah and I think about the day of writing ahead. I decide I *have* to implement the Principles.

They may not lead me to a sign from Sarah and they may not repair my drive to write, but they're a clear set of instructions on how to climb out of my rough patch. "How-to" instructions that work. As Anthony Robbins would say, I'm going to "model" my old self.

"Modeling" is one of those self-help concepts that's been around for centuries. It used to be called "mentoring" and, before that, it was called "apprenticing." It's a principle that's stood the test of time.

Cynical me says that Robbins and other modern gurus repackaged it as "modeling" so they could sell it again. But appreciative me says that they took a time-tested principle and made it fresh again so a new generation could benefit from it.

I step into my office and my plan is set. I'll implement the Principles from my notebooks and I'll get my career back on track. It doesn't occur to me that, maybe, this time around, I'm looking for something different.

16

I stare at the first Principle in my notebooks and I'm carried back to a distant place and time.

I'm on the other side of the grand canyon that divides my life. Sarah is still alive, laughing, and climbing the "ant tree" in our back yard. She named her favorite tree the "ant tree" because she'd discovered that ants marched up and down its branches, in tidy little lines, day and night, rain or shine.

I had never noticed the ants before but from then on, we were always checking to see if they were marching. They were, always.

I feel guilty for letting myself get transported back across that canyon, to where Sarah is still alive. It's not my world anymore. Sadness hadn't caught me yet. It hadn't dragged me down into the deadworld. Sarah is gone now and that feeling of wonder we shared, watching those ants forever marching, is gone too.

I tell myself that I didn't travel back across the divide to check on those ants. I'm here to retrieve the Principles. That's it.

I focus all my attention on the first Principle and I feel a sense of confidence. It's like I'm meeting an old friend who never let me down.

The first Principle was built on "thoughts," and both highbrow and lowbrow were on the same page when it came to "thoughts." They both believed that all knowledge was tied directly to the nature of thought. Self-help pioneers, modern gurus, philosophers, and scientists all validated this. And even though the Western canon didn't teach me what the keys to success were, it, too, validated this.

The early, self-help pioneers had their own versions of the first Principle. Their versions may have lacked intellectual heft, but I never had trouble figuring out what they were saying. They used clear and unambiguous language: Thoughts are things. You are what you think. Your thoughts determine your life.

But the most important version of the first Principle was my version. The one in my notebooks. The one that worked: *Control My Thoughts*.

This Principle played directly into my second Principle, so I turn my attention to it, too: *Focus My Thoughts On My Goals*.

After much trial and error, I'd added parameters to this Principle. My goals had to be clear and unambiguous. My goals couldn't be adorned with "ifs," "ands," or "buts." *No hedging*.

I flip forward in my notebooks and I see that I wrote down my goals and I focused on them every morning. That had been the first step to controlling my thoughts. I see that there's more to controlling my thoughts, but for right now, I do the critical thing.

I start.

I close my notebooks and, as I did back then, I write down my current film projects. Writing and selling those projects are my goals. Then I focus my thoughts on those goals and I don't let my thoughts wander. I *control my thoughts.*

17

Every morning, as soon as I get to my office, I focus on my list of projects. I won't describe what I'm doing as "visualizing," though that's what some self-help books call it. I'd describe it as concentrating my thoughts on my goals without letting any other thoughts interfere. It's a combination of words and images, with the key ingredient being the two Principles.

Unfortunately, this time around, the Principles aren't working. After a couple of weeks, my writing isn't flowing any better.

But I come up with a solution. All those years ago, when I first implemented the Principles, I had no problem with my writing. But I do now. So I add writing, itself, to my list of goals and I focus my thoughts on it, too. I tell myself that when I write, the world around me will disappear, like it did in the past. I'll lose track of time. I'll write with passion. And I'll find the drive to slog through the writing when that passion disappears.

I focus on my goals every morning, including writing. But after another couple of weeks, my writing still hasn't changed. So, I finally face what I've been avoiding. Something that troubles me about the first Principle.

It implies that a person can control the world. Self-help books spend pages and pages explaining this idea. They reveal and elucidate how thoughts can change the world. They cite personal, anecdotal, and spiritual examples. Some modern works go as far as using quantum physics to make this point.

But the one thing that Sarah's death has taught me is that, even though I can control my thoughts, I can't control the world. During Sarah's leukemia, I still believed I *could* control the world. I believed I could influence her leukemia. The Principle of controlling my thoughts was my way of life. It had lead me out of my rough patch and I thought it could also perform the miracle of curing my innocent daughter.

I truly believed that I could will Sarah back to good health. And since the odds were tilted so heavily in her favor, this conviction didn't seem like a long shot. The first Principle would cure her and that would be its greatest success.

I'm sure that this is the problem. The reality that my thoughts can't control the world is stopping me from implementing the first Principle with that same confidence I had in the past.

I go out for a walk and I end up on Olive Avenue, the street that borders Toluca Lake to its east. It has a view of Warner Brothers and I'm staring at the studios' large impenetrable walls. The tanned walls which shut out the rabble.

Some fellow writers and I call Warner Brothers "the heart of the coconut" because Hollywood is like a coconut. It's hard to break into, but once inside, it's full of sweet nectar. And Warner Brothers is the sweetest, richest part of the coconut, the heart of the coconut, because of its storied history.

A little bit of pride swells over me as I stare at the studios' walls. I've broken through that hard coconut shell many times. I've had deals at Paramount, Columbia, and the other studios. I've tasted that sweet Hollywood nectar. And right then and there, I realize that *this* is the only thing I'm asking of the Principles. I want them to work their magic again on my career and my writing. I'm not asking them to control the world. I'm not asking them to bring Sarah back. I don't remember any self-help guru claiming that he'd figured out how to resurrect the dead.

I walk back to my office, inspired by that little insight and, once more, I'm ready to forge ahead with my plan.

Back in my office, I write. My writing is halting. And over the next few days, the long slog continues with no reprieve. But I hang on to the idea that I'm committed to the Principles and I hope that I'll have a breakthrough.

Three days later, I do.

18

I get to my office and I focus my thoughts on my goals.

Five minutes in, I suddenly remember the most important part of the first Principle. A subtle part. A secret part. It's the part I'd discovered by sheer practice. By implementing the first Principle over and over again.

I open my notebooks and I whip through the pages, scouring them, until I find the secret part of my founding Principle. Then I immediately implement it.

There is a "me" who watches my thoughts. This "me" is separate from my thoughts. It pays attention to my thoughts. It controls my thoughts. *But* this "me" isn't my thoughts. *And* it's the only "me."

For my old self, this discovery had been the key to controlling my thoughts. Discovering this other "me" had been so profound an experience that I'd thought I'd stumbled into some kind of spiritual enlightenment.

I also remember feeling guilty about it. It had felt

sacrilegious to stumble into spiritual enlightenment when I was searching for the down-and-dirty keys to success.

I'd read enough Eastern thought to put my discovery into context. The barebones Eastern take on this other "me" was that he was beyond my ego. He was beyond the everyday machinations of my life. He was connected to the eternal. And if I allowed him to roam free in my life, my life would unfold without as much chaos.

During that rough patch, I was grateful to find this other "me." Not because I'd had a spiritual awakening or because I'd found a little more peace in my life, but because it confirmed the power of the first Principle. I was grateful because it played into the keys to success.

And now, I'm grateful again. Finding this other "me" is overwhelming. How could I have forgotten him? But the truth is, I hadn't forgotten him. I'd buried him. And the irony is that I find him again down here in my deadworld.

19

I spend the next few days controlling my thoughts with this "me" in charge. This "me" watches my thoughts float through my mind. He knows which thoughts to ignore, which ones aren't going to help me climb out of my rough patch. And as soon as I get the hang of it, I start to feel more empowered, more focused, and a little more at peace.

I'm still shrouded in the black cloud of death and I'm still looking for a sign from Sarah, but my concentration and my writing improves.

After a couple of weeks of focusing my thoughts, with this "me" freed from his burial plot, I see a change in my career. Momentum builds. Two pitches move forward. Multiple producers want to develop them and take them out to buyers.

I go back to my list of projects and I move these two pitches up my list and others down. This feels familiar. I'm using one of the Principles that appears later in my notebooks and I realize that it's time to implement more Principles.

I flip through my notebooks and I notice that, after I climbed out of that first rough patch, my lists of goals included more than just projects. They included financial goals.

I see that one of these financial goals was much greater than the others. Up to that point in my career, I'd had good years, but I'd never had a great year. I wanted a great year. The self-help books advised setting big, but achievable goals, and I'd thought that this goal wasn't that outlandish. I'd already had some good years and, at the time, spec scripts were routinely selling for big money. A "spec" script is a script that a screenwriter writes without being paid. A writer is speculating that someone might buy his or her script.

I'd also written a date under that financial goal. I'd given myself one year to achieve it.

I continue to flip through the notebooks and I unexpectedly land on the section where Sarah was diagnosed with leukemia. I'm dragged back across the grand divide.

20

Sarah was a powerhouse of a kid. Enthusiastic, energetic and happy, all the time. Then she suddenly changed. She became weak, unhappy, and cranky. She was sleepy all the time.

Her pediatrician thought that she might have an infection and prescribed antibiotics. But Sarah continued to be lethargic and the pediatrician continued to prescribe antibiotics, one round after another. None of the antibiotics were effective.

Meanwhile, I searched on-line for possible causes for Sarah's listlessness. I came across leukemia. It matched Sarah's symptoms. I mentioned this to Rachel and she thought I was crazy. She was right to think it. The percentage of kids who contract leukemia is tiny. Why would Sarah be one of those unlucky kids? Even I, an obsessive researcher, thought that was far-fetched.

But Sarah wasn't getting any better, so the next time Rachel took her to the pediatrician, Rachel asked for a blood test. The pediatrician gave Sarah a simple, "office visit" test and, an hour later, Rachel, Sarah and Jake were on their way to Cedars Sinai Hospital.

On the way, Rachel stopped at the Beverly Hills Public Library where I'd gone to write. She arrived just as I was leaving for lunch and she intercepted me in the dark parking garage.

I was shocked to see her. Why'd she drive out here instead of just calling me? *With* Sarah and Jake? I immediately asked her what was wrong.

She said, nothing was wrong. The pediatrician just wanted her to take Sarah over to Cedars to get some blood work done. She needed me to take care of Jake while she did.

We began to transfer Jake's car seat to my car and I asked her again what was wrong. What exactly did the pediatrician say?

She wouldn't tell me. She was in rush to get to Cedars and she kept repeating that Sarah needed to get that blood work done.

Finally, with Jake secure in his car seat, I said, slow down and please tell me what's up. Why are you rushing Sarah to Cedars?

In that cold, dark parking garage, Rachel slowed down and told me that Sarah might have leukemia.

I don't remember what happened right after that. I don't remember what I said or what Rachel said. But I do have one vivid memory, so brilliant it hurts:

Rachel and Sarah pulling out of that dark parking garage, leaving Jake and me behind. Our old, orange Volvo, which we'd bought used when we first moved to L.A., sweeping out of the gloom and into the sunshine of L.A. The sunny L.A. that had suddenly betrayed us. The L.A. where Rachel would have to fight a four-year battle to save our daughter from a relentless enemy.

21

Eventually, I resigned myself to accepting that bad luck had struck our family. The first year was an endless series of chemotherapy treatments, blood transfusions, terrible infections, and emergency hospital visits complete with lengthy stays.

From my notebooks, I'm reminded of the strange and upsetting dichotomy in my life back then. A bizarre disconnect between my personal life and my career. During all of Sarah's treatments, during the rest of her short life, my career went well. But I had a hard time accepting that. I felt guilty. My income and my health insurance were critical to Sarah's health and to our lives, but it still felt wrong to experience success while Sarah suffered.

I wonder if that dichotomy still resonates now. I wonder if that's part of my *new* rough patch.

I close the notebooks, but my thoughts stay back there. They swirl around one specific memory. A vicious blow. A brutal collision between my career and my personal life. I've tried to forget it, but I've never been able to. How could I?

First, an ugly truth about Hollywood. People in the business don't reach out to help. They actually do the opposite. They shrink away from tragedy, thinking it might infect them. Of course there are exceptions, and I've been lucky enough to work with some, but the business just doesn't attract caring people. And I'm not excluding myself from this generalization. If I'd been a caring person, I wouldn't have been attracted to Hollywood in the first place. I just hope that I've improved over the years.

But that ugly truth is the reason I didn't tell most of my colleagues about Sarah's leukemia. I told only those people whom I believed weren't going to run away from me. Unfortunately, I didn't know that someone in the business, someone whom I thought was on my side, was telling the whole town about Sarah.

Tom Saunders and I were having lunch in a small restaurant on Melrose. He'd picked a restaurant that hadn't yet been discovered by the industry, so the atmosphere was relaxed.

Tom was a producer who had set-up a script of mine. "Set-up" means sold. It means that I've been paid for my script. It *doesn't* mean that my script will get made and that's what Tom and I were talking about. What should I focus on in the rewrite to increase the chances of getting it made?

Tom thought I should focus on making the lead character more attractive to an actor. He wanted me to make the lead's emotional transformation, what screenwriters call the character's "arc," more distinct.

After Tom and I had dissected the lead character and decided a few ways to improve his arc, he asked me what else I was working on. In Hollywood, if a writer isn't working on projects other than the one he's meeting on, he isn't valuable. No studio or producer wants to be the only employer of a particular writer. They want validation that they've hired a writer whom others think is talented.

I filled Tom in, balancing hype with humbleness, until I saw that he felt reassured. But within seconds, that reassurance disappeared and was replaced by anxiousness. I was confused.

As the busboy cleared our plates, Tom appeared to be bracing himself. As if he were planning to deliver some bad news.

When the busboy left, Tom took a deep breath, then told me he'd heard a rumor. He'd heard that my daughter was sick and that I was no longer in the business.

I was stunned. I couldn't respond. I'd separated my home life from my career so thoroughly that I never expected them to collide over lunch on Melrose.

Tom must've have felt compelled to fill in the silence because he continued on, with a kind of hopeful, anxious laughter. Hopeful that my daughter wasn't sick. He said that this could only be a wild and unsubstantiated rumor. Obviously, I was still in the business. We were working on this project.

Still staggered by the blow, a question began to form in my mind. Who was spreading this vicious rumor? Not the part about Sarah being sick. But that I was no longer in the business. Who was vicious enough to spread this rumor at the very moment when my family needed me in the business more than ever?

I gathered myself and told Tom that the first part of the rumor was true, my daughter had leukemia. His heart went out to me. He was truly moved. Tears fell from his eyes, and he turned and wiped them away.

I told him that Sarah's prognosis was good. I didn't want him to feel bad. *And* I didn't want him to run away from me. I parroted the great survival rate for childhood leukemia. At the time, I believed in those survival rates, so I probably sounded convincing. I believed that Sarah would be cured. It was only later, after I'd dug deep into those survival rates, deep into the raw data from which they were calculated, that I'd discovered that this picture wasn't so rosy.

But I painted that rosy picture for Tom, and then I asked the only question that mattered. Who'd told him this?

I hid my anger, but I guess he could tell that I wanted to pummel whoever told him because he avoided answering the question.

I wanted an answer. I was sure that this person was keeping me from getting work. I could hear executives all over town saying that I'd left the business. I could see them crossing me off their lists of writers.

But Tom wasn't going to name the villain, so I had to decide whether to press him.

Tom was an A-level producer and he wasn't used to being pressed by anyone in Hollywood, especially a writer. Simply put, when it comes to feature film writers, we're on the bottom of the Hollywood totem poll.

Emily Parker, a famous actress, told me a great story that sums this up. Over the course of her career, she'd met hundreds of times with studio execs to go over the scripts she was to star in. And during every one of those meetings, the execs listened attentively to her suggestions about the script.

Then years into her career, Emily sold a script that she, herself, had written. When she met with studio execs as a writer, none of them listened to a word she said. Everybody else's suggestions, including those of the interns, were considered more valuable than hers.

I decided to throw off the shackles of being a feature film writer and I pressed Tom. I asked him, again, who the villain was.

And this is where Tom showed his true colors. He's one of the good guys and I witnessed this during the rest of Sarah's illness. Before every meeting, he'd ask me how she was doing and he didn't change the topic after I answered. He talked about her and asked me questions about her and always volunteered to help if he could.

Tom was also one of the few people in the business who came to Sarah's funeral. People whom I'd worked with for over a decade couldn't make it. They sent their apologies and excuses, while he, who I'd known for only a couple of years, rescheduled his trip to Europe so he could drive out to a small church in the Valley, and let me know that I wasn't alone.

Tom understood why I had to stop this rumor. I needed to work more than ever. He told me who the villain was.

I was staggered.

The villain was Mark Steiner, an agent at my very own agency. Mark wasn't my agent, but he worked with my agent. *My own agency* was telling the town that I was out of the business when I needed to work more than ever.

I didn't order coffee or dessert and neither did Tom. He could tell that all I wanted to do was get on the phone with my agent. We exchanged goodbyes and he told me that he'd keep Sarah in his thoughts.

I climbed into my car and called my agent, Ben Porter. His assistant said that he was on another call. I told her this was an emergency and she put me through.

I told Ben what I'd just heard and he acted shocked. I say "acted" because his anger felt phony from the get go. Ben was a company man. He worked for the agency and not his clients. His job was to placate clients and to keep them at the agency in case any of them turned into that rare cash cow.

Ben went into his "placate mode" and his feigned shock was part of his shtick. He said that he'd get "into it" right away. He promised to shut Mark down, the offending agent. He also assured me that this was all some kind of misunderstanding. Mark was a new agent and he was still learning the ropes.

I'd met Mark a couple of times so I knew he wasn't just learning the ropes. He'd been an agent for over a year and an assistant for four years before that. Mark wasn't some naïve country bumpkin.

After hanging up with Ben, I weighed whether to

call Mark directly and confront him. I'd never had a reason to call him. Now I did.

I called, but he didn't take my call.

A few minutes later, as I was pulling into my driveway, Ben called. He said that he'd spoken to Mark and he'd resolved the problem. Mark would be more careful in the future.

To me, that sounded like part of the "this was all some kind of misunderstanding" smokescreen, so I finally unleashed my anger. Ben fought back with, do you really believe that Mark was saying that?

Yes, I did. Because I believed Tom Sanders. I knew that Tom had understood exactly what he'd heard. I probably should've dumped Ben as my agent right then and there, but I couldn't. I had to keep working. Health insurance was more important than anger.

But from that moment on, I knew that Ben wasn't the agent for me. He didn't believe this was important enough to take a stand on. Instead, he'd protected his agency and hadn't admitted fault. It was all some kind of misunderstanding.

During the rest of Sarah's illness, I felt like I was fighting this lie. That it was keeping certain people, including my own agents, from considering me for certain jobs. Of course, I knew this might not be true, that I was being paranoid, but one thing *was* true. Some people in the business *were* running away from me.

22

Over the next few weeks, I resist diving further into my notebooks. I know that I have to extract the rest of the Principles, but I fear running into another old memory, so, instead, I implement the Principles that I've already excavated, and I spend most of my time working on the two pitches at the top of my list. This pays off.

An A-level producer commits to one pitch, which means he'll "brand" this pitch as his. This "attachment" is a huge coup. It validates the pitch for buyers. It says to studios and production companies that someone who's had tremendous success believes in the pitch and this makes it more likely that the studios will consider buying it.

Some producers do more than brand a pitch. Some help writers develop their pitches and scripts. If a producer is good at development, he or she can mold a story into something greater than the story that came out of the writer's cave. In many cases, a producer hands off the development of a pitch or a script to his or her executives. So the quality of development depends on the skills of those execs. Regardless, a writer always does the heavy-lifting.

"Heavy-lifting" is the hard work of crafting a coherent story based on a set of notes on an *existing* story. It's like adding new sections to a building after it's already been built, then trying to make it look like the building had never been remodeled. Sometimes a writer ends up tearing down the entire building and starting again. That's why it's called "heavy-lifting."

A day after I get this producer attached to my pitch, I get this red-hot production company attached to my other pitch, which is an idea for a TV series. Gary Rivers, the producer who runs the company, loves the pitch and says that he can sell it to a network. I've never sold a TV series, so this adds to my excitement. It looks like I've started climbing out my rough patch.

So with these two pitches ready for market, I decide it's time to add more Principles.

23

I dive into my notebooks and I find the next Principle. The Principle of Energy.

Self-help pioneers called this kind of Energy the life force, the universal mind, the collective unconscious, vitalism, electromagnetic energy, the etheric, flow, God, the divine, etc. George Lucas called it "The Force."

Some self-help pioneers did their best to quantify this Energy, but by doing so, they lost their credibility, especially for modern readers. Their definitions came across as antiquated and, in some cases, as quackery. But their guidance about using this Energy held up.

In my notebooks, I find that after I'd read a variety of works about this Energy, I decided I wouldn't be so arrogant as to try and define it. Instead, I would learn to recognize it, read it, and implement it. I'd learn to wield it in the battle for success.

I came to divide it into internal Energy and external Energy. I learned to read each kind of Energy as it applied to my projects and I used these "readings" as a guide. Depending on the Energy that surrounded each of my projects, I moved them up and down my master list. Then I'd divide my time among my projects based on where they fell on this list. The top projects received the most writing time.

To read this Energy properly, I had to ignore my emotions. The Energy surrounding each project had to be read objectively. This was tough to do and what made it even tougher, was that I wasn't supposed to ignore the strongest emotion of all. Passion.

I had to subtract all other emotions from my readings, but still gauge my level of passion because passion was a measure of the inner Energy that surrounded my projects. It couldn't be ignored like my other emotions.

There's more in my notebooks about reading Energy, but before I read further, I notice that as soon as I'd implemented the Principle of Energy, I landed my first book adaptation. And it happened in a nanosecond.

An exec whom I'd worked with years prior called me out of the blue. He'd started a new job with a producer and the producer was looking for a writer to adapt a book. The exec wanted to know if I was interested in pitching a "take" on it. (A "take" meant how I'd change the book so it could be adapted into a film.)

I didn't dillydally. The Principle of Energy dictated that I follow up immediately. Reading the external Energy on this project went like this:

This exec came to me with the book, thinking that I was a good fit. And he wanted to prove to his new boss that he could move a project forward. And his boss loved the project. *And* I didn't have to sell myself. The door opened for me without my having to kick it open.

Reading the internal Energy was easy. At this point, it only involved reading the book. I read it, loved it, and moved this project up my master list. Then, I put my time and effort into preparing my take on the book.

Days after that initial call, I went in and pitched my take. The exec liked it and wanted the producer to hear it. This strengthened the Energy even more. The exec set the meeting, I pitched the producer, he liked it, and he set the meeting with the studio. The next week, I pitched the studio and, three days later, I got the job.

24

I start applying the Principle of Energy to my current list of projects. I'm hoping to build on the momentum of the two pitches already moving forward and, maybe, land one of those "nanosecond" jobs.

I'm reading the Energy surrounding my current projects by using the guidelines I find in my notebooks.

For internal Energy, I gauge my level of passion for each project. This isn't a thumbs up or thumbs down kind of rating. It's more like a one to ten kind of rating, though it's not that precise. I don't assign each project a definitive number. I once tried that and it didn't work. I was trying to quantify the Energy and as I said earlier, that's impossible.

What I do instead, is gauge my passion for one project as it compares to another. Gauging my *current* passion is the key to this process.

Reading external Energy means evaluating the world's response to each of my projects. Is that exec or producer genuinely interested in my project, or am I the only person pushing it forward? There are times when it's okay if I'm the only person pushing a project forward. That's part of the internal Energy. But, at some point, a project has to attract fans or I won't be able to sell it.

I have to determine if a project truly has fans and if those fans can help it. They may like it, but they can't or won't do anything to move it forward. And this isn't necessarily a function of their level in the business. Sometimes having the lowest person on the totem pole attached to your project is better than having an A-level producer attached. He or she may champion the project all over town, while the A-level producer does nothing.

But there are no hard and fast rules. Sometimes having an A-level producer attached to a project, doing nothing, can work. You can use the producer's lukewarm interest to push the project forward, yourself.

On top of weighing these nebulous and fluid factors, I never have all the information I'd like and I never know whether that information is accurate.

The good news is that with practice, I know I'll become good at reading external Energy. I was good at it in the past. It's similar to the kind of process Malcolm Gladwell explored in his book, "Blink." When you process the information surrounding a project month after month, you're able to make instant evaluations. You can quickly gauge whether the external Energy surrounding a project is waxing or waning.

After applying the Principle of Energy to each of my projects, I reorder my list. The two pitches that are moving forward stay on top, but I do a much better job of ranking my other projects. That's critical because this list determines the amount of time I spend on each project. The higher a project is ranked, the more time I devote to it.

25

At home, I'm talking less and less about Sarah. Rachel wants to talk about her, but I avoid those conversations. I'm not obvious about it, I listen, but I change the subject as fast as I can. If I don't talk about Sarah, maybe the cloud of death will lift.

We have framed photos of Sarah scattered all around the house. I don't know how Rachel can move past them without being overwhelmed with sadness. I can't. I try not to look at them.

But there's something else in our house that makes me sadder than those photos. Sarah's coat has been hanging in our foyer since her death. I see it everyday as I walk in and out of our house. A fuzzy, warm, leopard-pattern coat that she wore everywhere. It was her armor against the endless pain the doctors inflicted on her.

One night, I decide to put that coat away. I take it from the coat rack and hang it in a closet. Thirty minutes later, Rachel sees that it's gone and she gets mad at me and we argue about it.

I confess that seeing that coat, so lonely, like the armor of a fallen soldier, makes me sad.

But Rachel says she loved it there. It made her happy to see it there. *Sarah loved that coat.* Rachel takes it out of the closet and hangs it back on the coat rack.

But the next day, when I come home, the coat is gone. I ask Rachel about it and she says that she put it away.

I ask her to take it back out. I feel like a big bully for hiding it in the first place and I apologize. *Please put it back where it belongs.*

Rachel tells me that she knows how much I miss Sarah and she embraces me. I wrap my arms around her and we stand in the foyer for a while.

I stare at the coat rack, now barren of Sarah's armor, and I don't know why I ever thought that hiding her coat would make me less sad.

The coat never returns, but memories of Sarah do.

Sarah loved Halloween and birthday parties. She loved swimming, climbing the ant tree, blue-raspberry sherbet, cold cheese sandwiches, and fruit platters. She loved her blanket "Pinky," her black, plastic rat "Precious," and the TV show, "My Time-Traveling Brother."

Sarah loved to act out elaborate stories. In one story, I'd play a dad who fell asleep in the middle of the afternoon. While I slept, my daughter, played by Sarah, would sneak out of the house and disappear. I'd wake up, find her missing, and I'd panic. I'd rush around the house, frantically searching for her, but I couldn't find her. Sarah would follow me around the house, giggling at my incompetence.

I'd end up having to hire a detective, also played by Sarah. The detective would ask me dozens of questions about my missing daughter. What did she look like? What was she doing before she disappeared? What were her favorite toys? Who were her friends? But I could never provide enough information and the detective would needle me about not paying attention to my daughter.

Finally, Detective Sarah would be left with no choice but to analyze the scant amount of information she'd gleaned from my pitiful answers. Using her brilliant deductive skills, she'd turn that information into clues and she'd start her search.

She'd hunt for my missing daughter all through the house, until one clue led her to a secret hiding place. Then, Sarah, my daughter, would run up to me and hug me, happy to be reunited with her dad.

I wish that detective could find Sarah now. I wish I could give that detective the clues that she needed. But Detective Sarah was right. I don't have enough information about my daughter. I never paid enough attention to her.

26

I arrive in my office and I focus on the Principles and on my goals. But before I start writing, I have to admit to myself that, even though my projects are moving forward, something is still missing from my writing.

I forge ahead anyway, writing solidly until mid-afternoon, and then I break for lunch. After lunch, I crack open my notebooks and find the next Principle, The Path of Least Resistance. I hope adding more Principles to my routine will restore my writing.

The Principle of The Path of Least Resistance (PoLR) is the most natural of the Principles. The Energy that I'm tracking, the Energy that powers, surrounds, and imbues my projects, is like the flow of water. And water always follows the path of least resistance. It flows along the clearest path. It avoids obstacles by going around them. Implementing PoLR means following that same kind of path.

When I first adopted this Principle, I had to overcome a built-in antagonism toward it. Like many people, I'd been taught, "No pain, no gain." I'd been taught that the only way to achieve success was to hammer through that thick, concrete wall in front of me. No one had ever said to me, "Hey, look at that door over there. Maybe you can just walk through it instead of banging your head against that concrete wall."

This Principle didn't negate hard work, but it said that hard work shouldn't be applied to hammering away at that concrete wall. It should be applied to following the path that flows most naturally. To finding that door and walking through it.

This Principle is also linked very closely to the Principle of Struggle vs Effort, but I don't skip forward to that Principle yet. Instead, I start to implement PoLR by evaluating which projects on my list have the best shot of moving forward with the least amount of resistance. Both the least amount of creative resistance and the least amount of business resistance.

When I say "least amount of creative resistance," I mean which projects are moving most easily from one stage of my writing process to the next. From idea to concept, or from concept to story, or from story to screenplay. If the project is a pitch, the third stage is story to pitch.

This *doesn't* mean that I drop projects that I'm having trouble with. At some point, all projects involve the slog, so I'd be dropping everything. But it does mean that I'll focus more time on the projects that are coming more easily.

And there's an added bonus to this process. When I

focus on projects that are going well, my subconscious has time to work on projects that aren't going so well. So when I return to those projects, the resistance is gone. If I give that other "me" inside my head time to solve a problem, he always comes through.

Applying PoLR to the business side of my projects means ordering them according to which has the best shot of making it out of my cave. Projects can't earn a living unless they migrate out into the world. The closer a project is to seeing the outside world, the closer it is to the top of my list.

The top of my list is made up of projects that are already out in the world, and I order those by evaluating the path of least resistance toward a sale. But a project that's been out in the world can still fall from the top of my list. Fans can turn against a project and adulation can turn into rejection.

The very top of my list is made up of projects that are set-up and earning a living. Those are the gold standard of projects. Unfortunately, there's no gold on my current list.

I finish rearranging my list and I stare at it. This list feels right. My agenda is clear. I'm headed in the right direction. So much so, that I decide to move on to the next Principle. The Principle of Action.

27

Some modern self-help gurus preach that a person can achieve his or her goals without taking action. They believe the only key to success is the "law of attraction." In short, this "law" says that you can achieve anything you want by focusing on what you want.

During my past rough patch, I tried this. It didn't work.

The early, self-help pioneers all believed in the Principle of Action. Modern self-help gurus probably conflated the Eastern traditions of sitting in silence, meant as avenues to enlightenment, with focusing your thoughts, a stalwart of the early, self-help pioneers, and came up with the idea that all it takes to achieve success is to sit around and wish for it. Who wouldn't want to buy into that?

For the early, self-help pioneers, focusing your thoughts was just one of their "how-to" keys to success, not the entire package. Even the classic get-rich-quick book, "Think and Grow Rich," lists thirteen principles for success. Its author, Napoleon Hill, captured his audience with that irresistible title, but he delivered his real advice inside his book.

Hill understood that a person couldn't just sit around and focus on his goals. A person had to take action. Hill saw that people were *designed* to take action. They were designed to communicate, to move, and to create. Al Bernstein, a sportscaster, once said, "Sometimes the fool who rushes in gets the job done." There's more truth in those ten words than in most modern self-help books.

From my notebooks, I see that I used a detailed approach to implementing the Principle of Action before it became second nature. I kept checklists of specific tasks that I'd try to accomplish every day. Tasks that would move my projects out of my cave and into the world. I kept a list of these tasks because this Principle was hard for me to implement.

I wasn't, and I'm not, a great salesman. But, in Hollywood, as in most careers, selling is part of the job. The quality of a person's work opens doors, but in the long run, meaning to sustain a career, that person still has to sell his work. *Even if his work speaks for itself.*

I've seen over and over again that Action is what differentiates working writers, directors, producers and all the other professionals in Hollywood from those with equal talent. All things being equal, Action is always the difference.

At the beginning of my career, years before I came up with this Principle, I saw the most sobering example of what happens if a person ignores it.

I went to a very competitive film school. The school was and is considered a gateway to Hollywood filmmaking. So it attracts ambitious students from all over the world and, when I arrived on campus, I found myself surrounded by talented classmates.

But one student was by far the most talented filmmaker in my class. His films were stunning. They were emotionally moving and visually dazzling. His writing, directing, cinematography, editing, and production design were superb. He outshone everyone in my class and my class generated many working professionals.

But this one student, who outshone us all, isn't anywhere to be found in the industry. Because Action wasn't his thing. Making his films was all the action he could bear, and even that was too much. He turned in every project late and some he skipped altogether.

I worked on some of his films, hoping that his talent would rub off on me, and during our long hours in the editing room, we talked about our Hollywood dreams. He told me that he was sure he was destined to become a well-known filmmaker. And he wasn't bragging when he said this. There was no arrogance in his tone or behind his words. Just pure faith and confidence in his work. The kind of confidence and faith that many self-help books urge people to manifest.

I believed him. His work reflected his talent. *His work spoke for itself.* It honestly did. But he never had a career. Not even for a second. Without action, talent wasn't enough. Without action, goals weren't enough. Without action, faith and confidence weren't enough.

In my notebooks, I see that after implementing the Principle of Action, I sold "The Curse," a spec script. That sale had been the biggest of my career and it'd signaled that I was most definitely out of that past rough patch.

I examine the Action "checklists" in my notebooks and I notice how much I'd expanded my contacts during that period. I made more calls, sent out more emails, went to more meetings, and did more follow-up than I ever had before.

But I had to force myself to reach out of my cave. That's why the checklists had gone on for over two years. The Principle of Action never became second nature. I stopped the checklists only because the Principle became a habit. At least for a while. But it, too, like the other Principles, eventually fell away.

28

I add the Principle of Action to my routine. I reach out to more people and I follow up on more leads. I also make the effort to call Ben, my agent, more often and I ask him to set more meetings.

I'm implementing the other Principles and I'm writing solidly every day. My writing doesn't flow as much as I'd like, but adding the new Principles is paying off in two ways. My projects are moving from one stage to the next more easily, and they're garnering more interest from the outside world.

I pitch my revised version of the TV series to Gary Rivers, the producer who runs the red-hot production company, and he signs off on it. He's ready to take it to buyers. Unfortunately, the holidays are about to start.

In Hollywood, the Christmas and New Year's break is absurdly long. Anywhere from five to eight weeks. Executives slow down way before the official holidays begin and ramp up slowly afterward. But they have no choice. In Hollywood, only a dozen people have the authority to make decisions and, during the holidays, these dozen people take long vacations. So the execs who work for them can't sign off on anything.

I tell Ben that I want to start pitching anyway, before the *official* holidays start. Before the two-week period that the rest of the country rightly acknowledges as the holidays. Would he please ask Gary to set meetings and would he do the same?

Ben was long ago initiated into the "long holiday" cabal, so he, too, slows down for five to eight weeks. He's in no mood to set meetings and he assures me that it's best to hold off until after the holidays. No one will buy a pitch right now.

This is the first test of my renewed commitment to the Principle of Action. I can literally take action and get the pitch out there myself, or I can wait. I know what my old self would've done. And that's what I do.

I call Gary and I tell him that I'm ready to pitch if he is. He's well aware of the long holiday tradition, so we talk about the risk of going out there now and it's clear from our conversation that he, too, doesn't want to wait. He instinctively uses the Principle of Action. That's probably why his production company is red hot.

Gary says that he's targeted four buyers for this pitch and he decides to set one of those meetings for before the holidays. He concludes that, if the pitch doesn't sell to that buyer, we might get some valuable feedback, and we can spend the holidays implementing it.

Gary sets the meeting and the next week we go in

and pitch. The meeting goes well, but Ben thinks we wasted one of our four chances. He says that the pitch will get lost in the network hierarchy as the decision makers head off for their extended vacations. Of course, he doesn't say this to Gary, just to me.

Three days later, Gary calls me and tells me that he heard from the network. They want to buy the pitch. I'm ecstatic. I've climbed out of my new rough patch.

29

Gary and I meet with the network. The execs on the project go through their notes and I retire to my cave to write the pilot script.

A few days later, I notice that I'm not as excited about my success as I would've been in the past. My excitement over a sale used to last three or four weeks, but this time, it's already dissipating. And what makes this even harder to explain is that I thought I'd be *more* excited than usual, not less. My career is back on track. The Principles have led me out of my rough patch. I have a paying job.

I begin to wonder if my enthusiasm is dampened because this is the first job I've landed since Sarah's death. It's now painfully clear that success isn't going to bring her back.

I work on the pilot and I continue implementing the Principles. For now, I don't add any more Principles and I try to avoid falling into the "lottery ticket" mindset. That's a sure way to end a Hollywood career.

When a writer sells his or her first script, he thinks

he's going to rocket to the top. He's won the lottery. Fame and fortune have embraced him. Just like he's read about.

But after he watches his first project stall out, and he's spent every last penny from its sale, he's forced to accept reality. He didn't win the lottery and that sale was exactly what it was advertised to be: His first sale.

Then he makes his second sale and he thinks, *this* is the ticket, *this* is the one. Same with the third sale and, maybe, even the fourth. It's only after he's watched a number of his projects either die a pauper's death or make their way to the silver screen without bestowing fame or fortune on him, that he realizes that this is a career, like any other career, and not a lottery ticket.

But no writer can shake this mindset completely, because Hollywood is the pure embodiment of America's general lottery ticket mindset. No one knows which projects will become hits and which will fail miserably. As William Goldman, the Academy Award winning screenwriter, once said about Hollywood, "Nobody knows anything." And that brings us to the biggest debate in town: How much of anyone's success in Hollywood is due to luck and how much is due to talent?

30

In Hollywood, the debate about luck vs talent lies just below the surface of every conversation. And when it's not below the surface, it's right out in the open.

My position is that it takes talent to get to a certain level, then luck takes over. In other words, it takes talent to get a writer into a position where he or she might get lucky.

I've debated my view many times, but one debate stands out because of my challenger's extreme position.

I'd met Roger Lewis during the 2007 Writers' Strike. He'd been the showrunner on "Betty," a much-loved sitcom that used to define American television. (A showrunner is the producer and head writer of a TV series.) Roger had found way more success in the business than I'd probably ever find. He'd won the lottery and I was sure he believed that this was all due to his talent.

After we got to know each other fairly well, the inevitable question came up, luck vs talent? Roger's view shocked me. He believed that his success, as well as everyone else's in Hollywood, was due to luck. And only to luck. It was hard to accept that he really believed this, but he argued his case well.

As a showrunner on "Betty," he'd read thousands of scripts from writers vying to land a slot on his writing staff. These scripts weren't just random scripts. They were scripts from the most successful writers in town. And what he saw in those scripts was a random mishmash of talent and complete lack of talent.

So Roger's argument was this: If talent had carried these writers to the top, then shouldn't the majority of these scripts have been good. These were the top writers in town. But the vast majority of these scripts were bad. This proved to him that talent wasn't required to make it to the top. It was all luck.

Roger wasn't arguing that some of these successful writers weren't talented or that he, himself, wasn't talented. He was simply saying that talent wasn't the reason for their success. Luck was. Otherwise, a vast majority of those scripts that he'd read would've been good.

I didn't have a great counter argument, except the old stand-by: It's also a matter of taste. Maybe *he* didn't like the scripts he'd read, but, objectively, they were good scripts.

He used that argument against me. Doesn't that mean that taste plays a big role in determining success, and if that's true, isn't that an argument for luck? A writer has to be lucky enough to get his or her script in front of someone who has the right taste for that exact material.

Roger's opinion is in the minority of one. Most screenwriters would argue for a combination of luck and talent when it comes to success. As I'm writing this, I notice a new thread on a private, on-line forum for Writer's Guild members. A newbie writer has just sold his first script and he's asking what he should do to ensure that this is the start of his career.

It's a newbie question, tinged with both arrogance and innocence. Arrogance because he thinks he's been chosen and innocence because he thinks it's within his power not to screw things up. Like he's been handed a lottery ticket and he's got to make sure he doesn't lose it.

I read through the advice given by the writers on the forum, working writers at all levels of the business, and it's a good compilation of advice on how to maintain a long career. But it's the kind of advice that applies to any career: Pick your battles. Stay true to yourself. Learn when to say "yes" and when to say "no." Learn to accept constructive criticism. Don't become cynical. Weather the storms.

I also notice that on everyone's list of advice is some reference, either directly or indirectly, to luck. They call it "chance" or "timing" or "making the right contacts," but it's always there. Yet every one of these writers, regardless of the length of their careers, doesn't dive directly into the grand debate.

Instead, they imply that if the newbie writer follows their advice, talent will win out in the end. That message is buried because these writers can't totally stand behind that argument. They've seen evidence that this might not be true but they don't want to pass it along. They don't want the newbie writer to believe that William Goldman might be right about Hollywood, "nobody knows anything."

In the grand debate over luck vs talent, Sarah's leukemia brought me closer to Roger's position. I believed that Sarah's leukemia was a random tragedy. Whether I unknowingly caused it or not, it was luck. Bad luck.

So why wouldn't I believe that success, like tragedy, is due to luck? Maybe in the back of my mind, I do. Maybe that's why I had stopped implementing the Principles back then. But if that's true, why I am implementing them now?

I remind myself why. Because they work. They *are* working. Just look at the TV pilot sale. They worked in the past and they're working now. This isn't the time to doubt them. This isn't the time to consider that it's all luck.

31

The writing on the pilot script goes well. I finish a draft and give it to Gary. He likes it, but has a few notes. I spend the next week incorporating his notes and the script gets better.

Gary likes the new draft and turns it into the network. A week later, he calls me and tells me that the network loved it and that we have a meeting with them to go through their notes.

After I hang up, I bask in the adulation. But I know better than to bask too long. I'm not going to fall into the lottery ticket mindset. I start working on one of my other projects.

Two weeks later, Gary and I are in the network meeting. We're surrounded by five execs, including an EVP (executive vice-president) and the meeting starts out with small talk. Gary has friends in common with the execs so the banter is gossipy and cheerful. The EVP joins in with a few jokes and an amiable mood is set.

Then we get down to the notes. The EVP and the execs unload a ton of them. This doesn't bother me.

"Notes" are a major part of a screenwriter's life. Screenwriters get notes on their script every step of the way. I take them in stride.

Before a writer shows his or her script to the town, he gets notes from his friends and confidants. Then he hands his script to his agent and his agent gives him notes. Then his agent sends the script to producers and they give him notes.

And if this writer is lucky enough to sell his script, he gets a round of notes from the studio execs and a fresh set from the producers. And if his script gets a greenlight, ("greenlight" means the script is going into production,) studio execs and producers give him more notes with the actors and director joining in the fun.

Notes continue all the way into production and through production, and the writer may even get notes after his film is shot because the studio may want to shoot new scenes.

My system for dealing with notes is based on recognizing whether a note addresses an element in my script that doesn't work.

Notes point to what I call "kinks" in a script and "kinks" refer to a character problem, a plot problem, a logic problem, or any of the myriad of problems that a script might have.

Job number one is to determine whether a note truly points to a kink or whether the note is an outlier. And this means that I have to be honest with myself. It's about the note and not the person giving it.

If a note points to a kink, then job number two is to figure out if that note also comes with a fix. If not, and that's usually the case, then I have to come up with the fix myself, part of my heavy-lifting duties.

After I get a set of notes, the next step is always to write a better draft. A draft with fewer kinks. Readers, whether they're execs or producers or directors or actors, expect as smooth a read as possible. Any kinks will throw them out of a script. And too many kinks, will throw them out permanently.

That brings me to Dan Felder, an executive who worked on the Sony lot. I liked Dan from the very first time I met him. I appreciated his brutal candor about the business and the straightforward way he dealt with me and with other writers. But what sealed our friendship was our very first notes session. Halfway into it, he leaned back, grinned, and said, "It's really just about that magic fairy dust, isn't it?"

This was so blunt a statement that it took me a second to realize what Dan was saying. He understood that the writers he worked with knew all the rules and formulas and he was acknowledging that there was another part to screenwriting. A part that couldn't be quantified.

Dan knew that regardless of his notes, the only thing that mattered was whether I could find that magic fairy dust and sprinkle it on my script. That magic fairy dust was what made a script sparkle with life. It made one script outshine all other scripts floating around Hollywood. It made a script sing.

If a script is sprinkled with that magic fairy dust, a reader will fall in love with it and champion it all over town.

32

I take my set of notes from the network and I sit down to rewrite my script. I'm looking to implement the network's notes and to smooth out as many kinks as possible. And if I'm lucky, I'll also find that magic fairy dust.

I spend most of my time rewriting the pilot and divide the rest of my time among my other projects. I also dive back into the notebooks, into the year where I'd reached my financial goal.

I'd made my big spec sale, "The Curse," and I was doing a rewrite on it for the buyer, Windstorm, a well-financed production company. They were high on the project and they were already talking about going into production.

Sig Rienfeld, an A-level producer, was attached to the project and his involvement meant access to top talent. So I quickly finished the rewrite to keep the momentum going, and I gave the draft to Sig. He liked it, had a few notes (as I said, notes every step of way), but he, too, opted to keep the momentum going and he gave the draft to Windstorm.

It's best not to put up roadblocks if a film is moving forward and Sig's decision not to make himself into a roadblock is one of the reasons he has a track record of getting projects made. He knew there'd be plenty of roadblocks up ahead and that there was no need to create one now.

The execs at Windstorm read the script that weekend and, on Monday, they called Sig and told him they loved it. Sig relayed the news to me and we both waited the rest of the week to hear more. But we didn't hear a peep.

After a month went by, I started to think that this was just another case of "we love it, *but...*" The "but" being anything from, we don't have the funds to finance the film right now, to, there's another film like this one coming out soon, so let's wait. I'd heard dozens of reasons for delay over the course of my career, so delay meant only one thing to me. It meant the death of "The Curse."

Six weeks later, I got a call from Sig. He'd finally heard from Windstorm. They were ready to make the film. I was shocked. I'd sold ten films, but only one film had actually made it all the way into production. So this was stunning news. It inspired me to refine my Principle and I developed TAERR, which stood for "Take Action, Evaluate Results, Repeat."

33

The Principle of TAERR was a refinement of the Principle of Action. I'd found that the actions I took didn't always generate the results that I wanted. But as the Principle of Action demanded, I still had to take action.

So TAERR said that, after I took action, I had to evaluate my results. If the results moved me closer to my goal, then I was to do more of the same. If the results didn't move me closer, I was to do something different. TAERR meant I was to do more of what worked and less of what didn't.

The hardest part to TAERR was being honest with myself about what was working and what wasn't. The key to implementing this Principle was not letting my own opinions, or the opinions of others, influence my evaluation.

I apply TAERR to my current actions and I like the results. The actions I'm taking are working and the sale of the TV pilot is proof.

But my actions aren't delivering results when it comes to my other big goal. Finding what's missing from my writing. I take some time to think about this. Is it possible that there's something about my writing that needs to change? My writing is delivering results. It's leading me out of my rough patch. But can it do more? Am I expecting it to do more? Is that the problem? Am I expecting it to help me climb out of my deadworld?

34

When I write, I use various methods for creating and developing a story. Separating "creating" and "developing" is one of those methods. In Hollywood, those terms are used interchangeably, but I've found that treating them as two separate parts of the writing process is a boon to writing.

"Creating" means writing a story from beginning to end, while "developing" means crafting a story *after* it's already been written. "Creating" means writing pure story, whether it's in prose form or in outline form, while "developing" means consciously applying the various techniques that I've learned for structuring a story. This includes, but isn't limited to, the three-act structure, the hero's journey, the eight-sequence structure, and the currently popular save-the-cat structure. It also includes my own paradigms based on reading thousands of scripts and watching thousands of movies.

So what more can I expect my writing to do, other than to create and develop a story? It's delivering on that level, career wise, but it still doesn't feel the same. Does that mean that I need to change the way I create and develop?

I think about that question and I suddenly remember something else that my writing used to do. It used to generate a feeling. A feeling that I haven't had for a long time. Euphoria.

I'd feel euphoria when I wrote. I didn't feel it all the time, but now, I don't feel it at all. Ever. Is that because I'm now living in a deadworld? Maybe there isn't any euphoria down here. But why should there be?

I picture myself as a character in my own story. A story that I create from my own life. And, just as with any story, I don't apply the paradigms yet. I just look over my story as it is, the pure story.

My life has a big act break, right there in front of me. Sarah's death. Her death sent me down into my deadworld and that points me toward a paradigm. I can develop my story by using the hero's journey structure, made famous by Joseph Campbell. I don't mean that I'm a hero in my story. I mean "hero" in the story sense, the main character.

The hero's journey paradigm goes like this: The main character leaves his familiar world and enters a new world. This new world might be dangerous, but it's always unfamiliar and extraordinary. Once there, the main character learns how to survive, and then sets out to accomplish a specific task. Along the way, he learns lessons about himself and about life in general. Then, transformed into a better person, he returns to his familiar world and leads a more meaningful life.

The hero's journey has other variations, complexities, and nuances, but that's the basic paradigm.

I've entered the deadworld. A world that's foreign and hard to navigate. A dark world, shrouded in random death. That part of the paradigm is clear.

I also see that my task is to find Sarah somewhere down here in the darkness. But I haven't seen her and I've been looking for a long, long time. It's also clear that I'm learning to survive here. The key to survival is accepting unhappiness.

But I don't see any lessons to be learned here, except how to get the hell out. In some stories, that's enough. Any screenwriter can point to dozens of films where the main character doesn't learn any lesson, except how to get the hell out of a threatening world. And that might be the case in my story.

I examine my story to see if any other parts of the hero's journey fit. But I don't try to twist my story into something it isn't. I use paradigms to *develop* my stories. Using paradigms to *create* stories drains the life out of them.

Maybe I'm not supposed to return to my familiar world. Maybe that part of the paradigm doesn't fit. Maybe my story doesn't have a happy ending.

35

The next morning, I focus on the Principles and on my goals, and then I work.

I write for a few hours and, as it gets harder to write, I think about the questions from yesterday. I think about euphoria. Maybe I'll never get that euphoria back unless I change my writing. But I realize that I have to implement all the Principles first before I evaluate anything or change anything.

I dive back into my notebooks and flip through them until I find the next three Principles. Think About Projects All The Time, Ignore Emotional Distractions, and Positive Conspiracy. Each of these Principles kept me on my upward trajectory after my big spec sale.

Now that I see them again, I notice that they're all related to focus. As I marched toward my financial goal, keeping my focus had become more critical.

Looking back, I now understand *why*. But it's a harsh truth to face. It proves that I'm an awful person. I know that I should face this head on, but I don't. Instead, I focus on the three new Principles. After all, they're innocent of any crime. I was the villain.

Think About Projects All The Time. This Principle referred to controlling my thoughts *after* my morning routine. In the morning, I'd focus on the big picture, my goals. But this Principle referred to the nitty-gritty, practical steps required to achieve those goals. It said that, during the rest of my day, I should think about the specific steps needed to achieve my goals. My mind shouldn't drift to other topics. The more I thought about these nitty-gritty details, the faster I'd achieve my goals.

Ignore Emotional Distractions. Implementing this Principle meant that I would try not to get involved in all the emotional maelstroms that arose around each of my projects. And there were a lot of these emotional maelstroms, so this was another tough Principle to implement.

Hollywood is made up of a good number people who have a lot of free time on their hands and they use that time to wreak emotional havoc. I'm generalizing, but it's safe to say that while other professions have a certain percentage of people whose jobs consist mainly of waiting, Hollywood probably has the highest percentage. People wait on drafts from writers, dailies from editors, notes from directors, budgets from line-producers, answers from actors, and hundreds of decisions that can only be made by the handful of people authorized to make such decisions, if and when they're available.

While people wait, they spend their time creating unnecessary battles. Ego wars, turf wars, and personal wars over slights, both real and imagined. And, when those battles break out, they eventually expand into the lives of those who do have a lot work to do. For those people, and there are plenty of them in Hollywood too, those battles are nothing but emotional distractions that suck up valuable time.

The problem is that these emotional maelstroms are so entrenched in the business that it takes years to realize that most of them will blow over, whether you get involved or not. But experience doesn't make it any easier to resist getting drawn into the maelstrom. Sticking to this Principle is tough. Mark Twain summed it up best, "I am an old man and have known a great many troubles, but most of them never happened."

Positive Conspiracy. The Principle was meant to counteract a certain way of thinking. Almost everyone has been ingrained with the idea that secret cabals are hard at work executing nefarious plots. Evil plots meant to do harm. Even when people's rational sides insist that this is crazy talk, it's always in the back of their minds. It's part of American culture.

Somewhere along the line, many people internalize these conspiracy theories and apply them to their own lives. They become paranoid. Not to a clinical degree, but to the point where they believe that people are actively trying to torpedo their careers.

This Principle said that, if I found myself thinking that some cabal was conspiring against me, turn it around and force myself to think that it was conspiring to help me. If I had to believe in a conspiracy, why not a conspiracy for good?

Long ago, right after I'd sold my first screenplay, Rick Blaylock, a screenwriter with an easygoing attitude, gave me some advice that applied to this Principle. Rick told me that no matter what I read or heard, rest assured that there was no "inside" to Hollywood. He said that everyone in Hollywood, whether they were wannabes or established, craved to be an insider. They craved to be part of this secret cabal. But there was no cabal. How did he know?

Because he grew up in what others would call the inside of Hollywood. George Blaylock, his father, was a famous Hollywood producer with a golden touch. A few decades ago, he had a twenty-year winning streak of box-office and critical successes. So when Rick was a kid, every major Hollywood player of the time drove up into the golden hills of Bel Air to hang out at his house.

And, at all those dinner parties, cocktail parties, and barbecues, he saw that these top Hollywood players, movie stars, agents, producers, writers, and directors, were all desperately searching for that cabal. He realized that if these people themselves weren't that cabal, then there wasn't any.

36

I look carefully at this section of my notebooks. I'm searching for any hint that I was aware of the awful truth that lurked inside these Principles. I don't find anything until I notice the project that sold right after I'd implemented these Principles. A project that moved me one step closer to my financial goal. That's where I spot the horrible truth. It's hidden inside that project.

I have always loved horror films with religious underpinnings. Films like "Night of the Hunter," "Rosemary's Baby," "The Exorcist" and "The Omen." And I'd always wanted to write a screenplay that would fit into that tradition, but I'd never been able to come up with a fresh story.

Then, after many years of failed attempts, I finally did. God would be the catalyst of my story, not Satan. My story would be a Christian take on a religious horror film. God would deliver a modern miracle to the world, but Satan would fight Him.

"The Secret of the Curse," my religious horror film,

was about Roy Hopper. He grew up in Virginia, where his father, a Baptist minister, sent him to Christian schools. Roy turned out to be a brilliant student, but he had doubts about God's existence.

When he was twelve years old, he and his dad were barbecuing in the backyard and his dad suddenly collapsed from a heart attack. Roy ran over to him and prayed to God to save him, but his dad died right there, cradled in Roy's arms. Roy lost whatever faith he had and, from then on, he was determined to use his intellect to debunk everything in the Bible. He eventually became a Columbia University archeology professor, and a hardened atheist.

When the script starts, Roy is in Israel, on an archeological dig, a dig that he believes will debunk the existence of one of Jesus' disciples. At the dig site, he uncovers an ancient Aramaic scroll that contains a sophisticated code. But when Roy tries to decipher this code, violent mythological creatures start to hunt him down. Creatures that he's forced to recognize as demons sent by Satan to destroy the scroll.

Roy finally deciphers the code and discovers that it's a computer code, a modern code, and it generates the most stunning video ever seen. A five second, grainy, shaky clip of Jesus Christ on the cross. He's staggered. He knows the scroll isn't a fake. Not only is he the expert, but it's been carbon dated. The computer code that generated this video of Christ on the cross was written over two thousand years ago.

In the end, Roy comes to believe in God and he delivers God's message to the world. He presents the video clip, a miracle for modern times, and he backs it up with proof that it's authentic. So unlike those classic horror films, this film was uplifting. God triumphed, not Satan.

I went out and pitched the project and I quickly got Tyler Gaverness on board. Tyler was an A-level producer known for making genre films that were also studio films. His involvement signaled that this film wasn't going to be a low-budget horror film.

We sold it on the third pitch.

"The Secret of the Cross" was a direct appeal to God. I was offering God the only thing I could, my writing, in return for my daughter's life. I had already offered Him my own life. It was a standing offer. Anytime he wanted to, he could cure Sarah and kill me. But He hadn't taken me up on that offer. At least, not yet. So I had tried this other tactic.

I would glorify Him to the Hollywood elites and, in return, He'd save my daughter. I wasn't asking that much. Sarah already had an eighty-five percent chance of survival. When I sold the project, I thought that God had taken me up on my offer. I thought that He'd cure her.

Now I see the awful truth buried in "The Secret of the Cross." This direct appeal to God had come out of my three new Principles. I was "Thinking about Projects All The Time." I was "Ignoring Emotional Distractions." And I was focused on "Positive Conspiracies." It's now clear that what I was really doing was ignoring Sarah's illness. And not just ignoring her illness, but ignoring her. Ignoring her life.

I wasn't spending those precious hours, those precious days, those precious months with her. I was working. These Principles were all about focusing on work and ignoring Sarah. *As she was dying.* And what makes this worse is that, as she was dying, she was full of life and joy. But I missed it. I was writing. I was making a direct appeal to God. And God was ignoring it.

37

I put down the notebooks and I look around my office and my eyes fall on a drawer that I never open. It's packed with scripts that I wrote many years ago. But it also contains something else. A file of Sarah's poems.

With the exception of "Goodbye, My Friend," the poem that Susie, my sister-in-law, wanted me to accept as a sign, I haven't had the courage to read any of Sarah's other poems. But the guilt of "Ignoring Emotional Distractions," and the desire to make amends, drives me to open that drawer, pull out that file, and randomly pick out a poem.

In the sky there is a spirit that created us,
Poor and rich,
High and low,
Sick and well,
Mean and nice.
These are the people He put in our world.

We will always be here,
Even after we are gone.

Tears well up in my eyes and my first thought is, *this isn't a sign.* I'm defensive because it very well looks like one. Sarah is talking about God because she knows I was just reliving my plea to Him to save her life. Is she telling me that He *did* save her life? Is she telling me that she's here even though she's gone?

At first, I don't remember this poem or where it came from, but then the memory comes flooding back. Sarah came up with it the summer before she died.

Grace Hailey, a minister and Rachel's friend, had invited us over to her rectory for lunch. After we ate, Sarah and Jake wanted to see the inside of Grace's church.

Grace was more than happy to let them explore and they darted up and down the aisles and checked out every pew.

After that fun ran out, Sarah marched up to the front of the church and stood next to the pulpit. She turned to face us, seated in the pews, and she started preaching. She recited that poem. Grace grabbed a pencil from a hymnal holder and wrote it down on an offering envelope.

In the sky there is a spirit that created us,
Poor and rich,
High and low,
Sick and well,
Mean and nice.
These are the people He put in our world.

We will always be here,
Even after we are gone.

When Sarah finished reciting the poem, Grace turned to me and said, "That's the most powerful sermon I've ever heard."

I have no idea why I can't accept that this is a sign. It's the second time Sarah has spoken directly to what I was thinking. Is she trying to tell me that God didn't ignore my plea? *We will always be here, Even after we are gone.*

I tell myself that these are just words. But her words move me and I see the irony of dismissing her poem as "just words." "Words" are what I do every day. I write word after word, thousands of words. And I try to find words that'll move people. I try to find words that will answer the question that every good story tries to answer. *How should I live my life?* And that's what Sarah was doing. She came up with some words to help me live *my* life. And now I'm dismissing those words. First, she told me why she had to go:

The boats are crowded.
The subways are packed,
The road is flooded.
My house has no roof,
The windows are cracked.

Then she told me that she wouldn't forget me:

I will remember in my heart,
How we skipped and jumped,
And played together.
I will love you forever
But now I must go.

And when that didn't take, like a good daughter, infinitely wiser than her dad, she tried another tactic:

We will always be here,
Even after we are gone.

If I can't accept that she's gone, then she's telling me to accept that somehow she's still here. She told me that she still loves me and, if that's not enough for me, then she's sticking around to prove it. Is it possible that this is a sign? It can't be.

I put the poem away.

I look at the Principles and I tell myself that they worked regardless of the awful truth. *I didn't mean to ignore you, Sarah.* I needed to focus on earning a living. For your sake.

I think back to Sarah's funeral. Grace, the minister, who heard Sarah recite those moving words, gave the eulogy. Grace spoke about Rachel's bravery and fortitude. How Rachel fought side by side with Sarah. How she was always there for her. How she gave her entire life over to her.

Then Grace mentioned me. One time and briefly. She said that I worked quietly and diligently to support my family without expecting any recognition. She said that I did what I had to do. That I played my role. But the awful truth is that it wasn't the right role. It wasn't the role that was called for. I was busy "ignoring emotional distractions."

38

I add the three new Principles to my daily routine and I ignore the awful part. It's right there in the Principles, "Ignore Emotional Distractions." But I don't ignore that Sarah's gone. That's callous and insulting to her.

Many self-help books list examples of successful people who've overcome tragedies. These stories serve as inspiration and motivation. But they never mention how these people actually dealt with their tragedies. Abraham Lincoln, JFK, Mark Twain, Robert Frost, and many others lost their children. Did they ignore their loss to the point of being callous? Or did they just ignore minor emotional distractions?

I don't know what they did, but I know I can't ignore Sarah. It may be too little, too late, but I won't ignore her.

After only a couple of weeks of adding the new Principles to my routine, I see results.

I turn in the rewrite of the TV pilot and the network EVP loves it. Not only that, but Gary Rivers, the producer, tells me that of the nine pilots originally being considered for production at the network, only three are still in the running and mine is one of them.

And another one of my projects suddenly leaps forward. Bill Goode, a producer that I've worked with on and off, calls me out of the blue and tells me that he just had a meeting with a production company that has money to buy projects. He brought up an old pitch of mine and they liked the concept and want to hear it.

Bill asks me if it's still available and I tell him that it is. He says he'll set the pitch meeting.

Bill and I had tried to sell this pitch many years ago, but the external Energy waned and it never sold. It eventually sunk to the bottom of my list, though it never fell off. Internal Energy kept it alive. It always elicited some tiny spark of passion.

Now, external Energy has weighed in. The next morning, I move the project up my list.

A week later, Bill and I go in and pitch the project to the president of the production company. He loves it, but not enough to buy it. I expect that to be the end of it. It usually is.

But a couple of days later, I hear something that I don't expect. The president of the company loves the concept and can't get it out of his head. He loves the core idea, but not the story I created around that idea. He'd like to hear another take.

Now comes the dilemma. In this case, coming up with another "take" is a Hollywood euphemism for "we'd like you to work for free." The production company could've opted to buy the story I already had, which means that they'd be buying the concept too. I would then create a new story before going to the script stage. That scenario isn't unusual. I've sold three projects that way. The benefit of that scenario is that I get paid for working on the new takes.

But this production company wants me to spend weeks on a new take without knowing if they'll step up to the plate with a check. That scenario isn't unusual either. It's up to me to decide if working for free on this project is better than working for free on another. Which effort is more likely to lead to a paycheck?

My former self wouldn't have hesitated to work for free in this particular case. Bill, the producer loves the project and I love the project. And the potential buyer, the president of this company, loves the project. The Energy is all positive.

In the past, I would've sat my butt down in my chair and written a new take. But this time, it isn't so clear-cut. What's different? It's that nagging feeling that something isn't quite right. Everything is moving forward and my career is back on track, but the Energy doesn't feel as positive as it should and my writing isn't the same. It doesn't feel like it did when I climbed out of that first rough patch. This time around, I never feel euphoria.

39

A couple of days later, Bill Goode calls me and he wants to know if I'm going to work on that new take. I tell him I don't know yet and he takes that as a "maybe" which any three-year-old can tell you means "no." But Bill doesn't respond like a three-year-old. He doesn't throw a fit like many in Hollywood might. And he doesn't give me the hard sell.

He believes that the way a project comes together influences the way it plays out. If people coalesce around a project of their own free will, rather than through coercion, then that project has a much better chance of breaking through all the roadblocks that lay ahead. And that philosophy has served him well. He has great credits under his belt.

So instead of the hard sell, Bill tells me that he can't guarantee the production company will buy the project, but he does believe that the president of the company truly loves the idea. He says that if I decide to work on one project for free, this one is worth a shot.

Bill's attitude adds more positive Energy to the project, but still not enough for me to say "yes."

Another project moves up my list. This one takes place in the Los Angeles of the thirties and forties, so, for guidance and inspiration, I scour through photos from that time period, and after exhausting the Internet, I head over to the Beverly Hills Public Library, which has an excellent collection of photos of old L.A.

I like the Beverly Hills library, a grand and open building, but I still have a hard time walking through its parking lot.

I park and this time is no different. I walk through that cold, dark structure and I can't help but see Rachel and Sarah in our old, orange Volvo, pulling out of this gloomy garage, heading into battle.

I'm happy to step out into the sunshine.

In the library, I request photos from the special collection and, as I wait, I weigh whether I should work on that new take.

The photos arrive and I study them. Within minutes, I'm lost in the L.A. of the past. Clean, wide boulevards, bright bungalows, restaurants and businesses dressed in spiffy, art-deco regalia. L.A. in its glory days, full of hope and promise and fresh glitz.

I should be studying the photos of downtown L.A. since that's where my project takes place, but I'm drawn to the studio photos. I would've loved to work in the old Hollywood studio system.

In the thirties and forties, almost all screenwriters were hired as full-time employees of the studios. Screenwriters weren't freelancers, hoping to string together enough jobs to have a career. Sure, they hoped their contracts would be renewed, but, while under contract, they weren't worried about generating new projects to sell.

During this Golden Age of Hollywood, the creative and the business parts of studio filmmaking were perfectly integrated. Hollywood was a factory town of blue-collar workers and blue-collar included writers, directors, and actors. Some may have been stars, but all were part of the blue-collar workforce that reported to the factory and generated the best films of all time.

In today's Hollywood, feature film writers fall into four groups, consolidated in the Writer's Guild of America. This is the blue-collar workforce that powers what's left of the studio system. But instead of working on studio lots with other writers, which created a camaraderie among them that's totally absent from today's Hollywood, these writers toil in isolation.

Unemployed writers make up the largest group in the Guild. These are writers who haven't worked for years, but, at some point in their careers, they sold at least one project to a Guild signatory. Sporadically employed writers make up the second largest group in the Guild. These writers don't work consistently, but they periodically sell a script or get hired to write a project.

The third group of Guild screenwriters is small. It consists of the journeymen writers who are constantly employed. They do the bulk of the writing in Hollywood, without fame and usually without fortune, and most of their scripts don't get made.

The fourth group of screenwriters is also small and it's made up of the writers that people associate with screenwriting, if they think about screenwriting at all. These are the writers who are "famous," within the Hollywood community and sometimes outside of it. These writers work the most and make the most money.

I belong to the third group and, believe me, even with the negative appellation that I've slapped onto this group, "journeymen," it's a small group and I'm happy to be a member.

Many in town diss the "journeymen" appellation because they associate it with its secondary definition, "an experienced and competent, but undistinguished worker." But it's an appropriate appellation because of its primary definition, "one who has served an apprenticeship in a craft and is a qualified worker in another's employ." To sustain a career as a screenwriter, a writer must meet the criteria of this primary definition. That's because regardless of what the greater Hollywood community thinks, buyers in Hollywood think differently. *They don't diss journeyman, they hire them.*

A vast majority of the time, buyers hire journeymen when screenwriters from the "famous" group aren't available. And when buyers hire writers from the "famous" group, they're also hiring journeymen, because ninety percent of the writers in that group are journeymen too.

The "X factor" is always that magic fairy dust. No one can predict that part. But by hiring a writer "who has served an apprenticeship in a craft and is a qualified worker," buyers are upping the odds that they'll receive a good script.

40

I'm staring at a black and white photo from the forties. It's a glossy photo of screenwriters on the Paramount lot. They're sipping coffee on the porch of a writers' bungalow. That bungalow is still on the lot. I've been in it. It's now populated with producers, not writers. I'm imagining that these writers, these factory workers, are hammering out a plot point or discussing what "picture" they hope the studio assigns to them next.

As I'm pining away for the good old days, when writers worked on the lot and not in their caves, someone says "hi" and I'm ripped out of Hollywood's Golden Age. I turn around and a guy in his late twenties, stubble-faced, wearing jeans and a T-Shirt, smiles at me. He's hauling a shoulder bag and I have no doubt that inside that bag is a laptop. I'm certain that this guy is a screenwriter.

He says, "You probably don't remember me, but we talked at Priscilla's." He's right. I don't remember him. But prior to getting my office, I used to divide my time between writing at home and writing in coffee shops. Including Priscilla's in Burbank. So I believe him when he says we met there.

I've been approached dozens of times by wannabe writers. It's part of the L.A. landscape. If a newbie writer is in a coffee shop and he suspects that he's watching a working screenwriter write, he'll approach that writer hoping for a sliver of advice or, better yet, an introduction to an agent or producer.

Some working writers brush these wannabes off. Others are glad for the attention, and talk to them, *then* brush them off. A few give these newbies advice and even agree to read their scripts. Whether or not a working writer is approachable has nothing to do with his or her stature in the industry. I know screenwriters who've sold one script, who never talk to newbies, and I know established writers who'll gladly talk to any and all newbies.

I've always been approachable. But because of that, I know that most "random" screenwriters aren't good writers. And when they ask for advice, I want to tell them to pick another dream. But who am I to judge?

So, instead, I give them what they want. Notes on their scripts and career advice. And I hope that their writing improves. But if it doesn't, there's always luck. And if Roger, the showrunner, is right, luck might be enough.

I turn my attention from the photo of the bungalow to this newbie writer. He tells me that he admires my success and he rattles off some of my credits. I'm impressed. He had to do more than perfunctory research on me to find my credits because they consist of unproduced films.

I know that he's trying to ingratiate himself with me, but it's still working. Not because he's treating me like I'm part of that "famous" group of screenwriters, but because his easygoing banter is a good indication that he's firmly rooted in reality. This doesn't mean that he's a good writer, but it does mean that he's probably not a psychopath.

As we chat, I feel torn about getting involved. I don't want to end up giving him false hope. A friend of mine used to joke that cars should drive up and down the streets of L.A. with bullhorns blaring out, "Go back to where you came from. Go back to your towns and villages. There is nothing for you here." He felt that Hollywood was handing out too much false hope.

After a few more minutes of chatting, the newbie asks me if I have time to grab a cup of coffee. I say "yes" and, as we head over to a coffee shop just outside the library, I'm asking myself why I said "yes." I don't have a good answer.

We buy our cups of coffee and sit down. With bright eyes, he fills me in on what he's been doing since we last met. His tales are a series of attempts to get his scripts read, and a series of close calls where his scripts were read, garnered interest, but that interest didn't result in an option or a sale.

He's so excited about screenwriting that, as he recounts his adventures, pure joy pours out of him. It's also clear that he believes, with unshakable faith, that talking to me is going to bring him one step closer to realizing his dream.

As he continues to regale me with his tales, I recognize that what I'm seeing and listening to aren't just stories, it's passion. This writer's passion to "make it." His bright eyes radiate a fierceness to be validated. That same fierceness that I see all over town, from the smallest, dingiest offices in East Hollywood, to the biggest, brightest bungalows on the Paramount lot. I realize that I, too, used to radiate that passion and fierceness. I wonder if I still do. Or has losing Sarah killed that?

My mind now starts to jump around, trying to make connections to what I'm feeling. Connections from the deadworld to this living world. I'm getting my career back on track and somehow I can't connect it to Sarah's death. To her life. To a sign. To passion. To euphoria. To crushing sadness.

Then my thoughts suddenly stop jumping around. They come together, just like that. I don't have those "bright eyes" anymore because I'm not concerned about making it. I made it. I made it more than once. More than twice. I made it many times. And I'm making it again. It's not Sarah's death that killed my passion and fierceness. It's making it that did. Is that why my writing isn't the same? Is that why I'm expecting more from my writing this time around?

The newbie writer tells me about this new script he's just finished. I listen to the premise and I give him some story advice. I also tell him which producers might like the script and I suggest ways to approach them.

He loves the advice and he's so thankful that his

eyes tear up. But when I see those tears, I want to do an about-face. I want to tell him that screenwriting isn't all it's cracked up to be. Don't pursue it. Find something more meaningful and stable. But I know that coming from me, this would sound like I think I'm better than him. Like I'm telling him to give up his dream while I had pursued mine.

So I don't tell him to give up his dream. Instead, I continue to give him the names of producers who might like his script. When he leaves, he's as happy and moved as I've ever seen anyone.

Then I head back to the L.A. of the thirties and forties and I realize that I'm feeling pretty good myself. I don't know why I said "yes" to sitting down with this random writer, but it turned out to be the right move. I think I'm closing in on some answers.

41

I get up the next day, concentrate on the Principles, and before I start writing, I've made a decision. I will develop a new take on that pitch, which I'm now calling "Buggs Lake."

I call Bill Goode and tell him. He's pleased and he wants know what convinced me to move forward. I tell him that I was inspired, which is the truth, but he thinks I mean "inspired" as in creative inspiration. He thinks I came up with a great idea for a new take. But I was inspired by the Principles. This morning, as soon as I finished focusing on them, I knew that it was time to move forward with "Buggs Lake."

I start working on it, jotting down a few ideas, and I quickly latch on the beginnings of a new story. I spend the rest of my day expanding that story.

When I come home that night, Rachel tells me that she's ready to go back to work. She wants to get a part-time job. I'm against it, but I'm not sure why. I know she's been going to her grief group less frequently and that she's been spending more time volunteering at Jake's school, so I ask her if the volunteer work isn't enough.

She says that she needs a job. Her life doesn't feel in sync without a job. She's worked her entire life, starting in middle school, through high school and college, all the way up to Sarah's illness. She wants to know why I'm against it and I answer that I want her to spend as much time with Jake as possible. He missed his mom for four years and he deserves to hang out with her now.

I can't honestly say that this is the real reason I'm against it, I don't know the real reason, but I say this because I know it'll make her feel guilty. It does.

We argue and, during the argument, I find out that she's beginning to feel like I do about Sarah's death. She's not going to "get over it." Ever. She's living with it and she's accepted that this overwhelming sadness will always be with her. She's accepted the hole in her heart. But unlike me, she's decided to move forward with her life and carry that sadness with her.

As she tells me this, I wonder if the hole in my own heart is the biggest part of my heart, as if there's no heart there at all. Just an empty, dark space where my heart once was. I wonder if that's why nothing feels right. We all need a heart.

I don't relent on my opposition to her job, but one night she tells me that she sent her resume to a potential employer and that they want to interview her. We argue again, but I have to admit to myself, and not to her, that the job sounds great. It's not a high-paying, corporate job like the one she left, but that's not what she wants. She feels compelled to do something different.

I still don't want her to go back to work, even if it's a different kind of job, but I know that I'm never going to win this argument. She *should* do what she wants. And she's being gracious enough to try and get me on board before she does.

For tonight, we agree that she'll go to the interview and that we'll talk about it, again, if she's offered the job.

As I'm lying in bed trying to fall asleep, I think about Rachel's wish to do something different. Right now, I'm trying to do the exact same things I did before Sarah's death. I'm literally "modeling" my old self.

But it's working. I've climbed out of my rough patch and my career is back on track, the same as it ever was. *Except* for one major part. My writing isn't the same. Maybe I, too, should be doing something different?

42

I'm now juggling five active projects and each has a lot of Energy behind it. But I still feel, as Rachel would put it, like I'm not in sync with my work. I feel removed from it and this becomes more obvious every time I try to implement one specific Principle, "Think About Projects All The Time." I can't focus on my projects all the time. Instead, I think about what's missing.

Someone once told me that joy can turn into tragedy, but tragedy can't ever turn into joy. My memories of Sarah fill me with unrelenting grief. But I don't ever want to forget her. I *want* to think about her. I *want* to remember *how we skipped and jumped and played together.* I *want* to ring joy from tragedy.

I want to fill the hole in my heart with memories of Sarah. But I want those memories to trigger joy. That's the opposite of learning to live with the hole in my heart. That's like trying to repair the hole. It's like pouring concrete into that hole, a concrete made of good times.

I decide to start filling that hole by looking at those photos of Sarah we have scattered throughout our house. The ones I've been avoiding, on the mantelpiece, on the piano, on the sideboard, and taped to our kitchen windows.

I wait until Jake is sleeping and Rachel is reading in   bed. Then I head toward a specific photo that I want to confront.

On the way, I check out other reminders of Sarah. I want to make sure that I haven't misjudged them. Maybe if I do more than glance at them, they'll trigger joy instead of sadness.

I stare at Sarah's lava lamp, the one she'd wanted so badly. I see her hugging it tightly, beaming, after she'd unwrapped it on Christmas morning. But then I remember Rachel rushing Sarah to the hospital that afternoon. Jake and I finished Christmas dinner alone.

I stare at Sarah's collection of snow globes and I remember the Saturdays that Sarah and I spent strolling through Farmer's Market, heading in and out of every tacky gift shop, examining every snow globe. I should've bought her all of them at once, rather than just one each Saturday. She had so few Saturdays left.

I stare at a picture that Sarah drew. It's all of us lying on a golden tropical beach, with blue dolphins leaping out of a bright green sea. I see the seaside vacation that we were never able to take.

I stop. I didn't misjudge these reminders of Sarah. I don't feel joy. I feel sadness.

I head for the photo that sits framed on the piano. It's the photo I avoid the most. I scoop it up and I sit on the couch and I stare at it.

It's a photo of Sarah and me at her school's Halloween fair. Halloween was Sarah's favorite holiday. In the photo, she's dressed as a witch, in a black lace dress and a gold witch's hat with prints of black spiders speckled across it. I'm wearing the traditional witch's hat, black, tall, and pointy. We're both staring into the camera, smiling. She's happy. I can see that.

I look at myself and I guess I'm happy too. I must've been. But I don't believe I could've been. I knew what was going on when this photo was taken. The leukemia was threatening to kill Sarah. She'd already had many, many treatments. She'd already suffered greatly. She'd lost her hair twice. The leukemia was winning.

I tell myself, she's happy. *She's happy that day.* But staring at the photo of her happy, makes me sad. It's a photo of loss. It's a photo that glosses over the brutal reality of random tragedy.

I try to bury my negative thoughts. I try to control my thoughts.

I stare at the photo and I tell myself that this is a photo of joy. Sarah *is* happy. There isn't any tragedy here. She's genuinely happy that it's Halloween and that she's healthy enough to go the fair. She loved that Halloween fair and she wasn't thinking about leukemia. She was thinking about what booths she wanted to visit and about heading into the haunted house.

I'm crying. This isn't going to work. Joy can turn into tragedy, but tragedy can't ever turn into joy. I'm staring at the proof.

43

I finish up my new take on "Buggs Lake." I pitch it to Bill, first, before we go back into the production company. He likes it and makes a few suggestions. I implement his notes and then we go into the production company and I pitch it to the president. He loves the new version and, the next day, he backs up his praise by stepping up to the plate. He buys the pitch.

I now have two paying jobs. The TV pilot and "Buggs Lake." It's rare for a working screenwriter to have more than one paying job at a time.

Screenwriters who belong to the "famous" group can land anywhere from two to four jobs at the same time, but that's not the case for other working writers. We're lucky if we can land two jobs simultaneously. I've had that good fortune a few times, but now, with the Principles working so well, I wonder if I can accomplish the unthinkable. Three jobs at the same time.

I'll have to ride this wave of good fortune carefully to have any shot at it. I remember that this is a

Principle too. Ride the Wave. So I dive back into the notebooks to find it.

The next set of Principles does include Ride the Wave. And I also find Struggle vs Effort and Don't Know, Don't Go.

Struggle vs Effort was the most important of this set of Principles, so I look at it first. It said that it's not just hard work that led to success, it was a certain kind of hard work.

Almost everyone is taught that the harder they work, the more they'll succeed. Their entire life, they're told that they'll have to struggle through long days, over many years and decades, to achieve success. No pain, no gain.

This Principle picked up where that advice left off. It actually defined what kind "hard work" lead to success. The key was separating Struggle from Effort. When a person struggles for a long, long time, the boundary between Struggle and Effort blurs and that's the problem. To move forward, that boundary needs to be reestablished.

Struggle is when every instinct and every emotion tells a person to stop whatever he's doing, but he continues anyway. Effort is timeless action. Effort is when a person losses himself in whatever he's doing. His focus is so concentrated that he doesn't notice pain or setbacks and, if he does, he doesn't care. He's lost in the action of trying.

Some call this "flow." Some call it "Zen." Some call it "The Way." Whatever it's called, it's usually the path to success. It's "right" action. It doesn't mean smooth sailing all the time, but it does mean that obstacles become guideposts, not concrete walls.

In my notebook, I find a saying by W.C. Fields that summed it up, "If at first, you don't succeed, try, try again. Then quit. No use being a damn fool about it." Struggle leads down the wrong path and Effort leads down the right path.

This Principle was a big part of my ascent out of that first rough patch. I knew that working long hours was part of success. Every working screenwriter wrote long hours. Same with other professions. Successful attorneys practiced law for years. Successful businessmen built their companies over years.

But I also knew that this wasn't the whole picture. If all a person had to do to succeed was work long hours, then everyone who worked long hours would be a roaring success. That wasn't the case.

The Principle of Struggle vs Effort connected hard work to success. It revealed that successful people didn't fight themselves during all those years of hard work. They put out tremendous effort, they endured tremendous hardships, but they didn't fight their instincts and feelings. They followed them. They chose the right path every step of the way. They felt in sync with their work.

I look over this section of my notebook again because there's something here that applies to me right now. It applies to that feeling that something is missing. It applies to my drive and to euphoria. Is it that I don't love what I'm doing anymore? That can't be it. I love writing. But it's not the same. Has it become too much of a struggle? Is that what's going on? Or is it the deadworld? Maybe writing will always feel different down here in the deadworld.

44

The next day, after I finish writing, I go back into my notebooks to see if Struggle vs Effort can shed some light on my writing. Instead, I end up tracking my old self's career.

"The Curse," my big spec sale, was moving forward. Windstorm, the production company, had given Sig Reinfeld, the producer, the okay to meet with directors.

"The Secret of the Cross" was also moving forward. The studio had asked me to water down the script. Ironically, they didn't want me to water down the horror or the violence. Those parts were fine. Instead, they wanted me to water down the intensity of the professor's faith at the end of the script.

In the first draft, the professor realizes that this grainy video of Christ on the cross is a real miracle. A miracle that speaks directly to our time from across two thousand years of history. He can no longer debunk Christianity. His faith is restored in a heartfelt epiphany.

But the studio wanted to leave some "doubt" on the

table at the end film. "Doubt" would make the film acceptable to the widest possible audience. The studio wanted this to be a mainstream film about faith, not a blatant validation of faith. Both Tyler Gaverness, the producer, and I had reservations about inserting this "doubt." So before I dove into the rewrite, we had another meeting with the studio.

In the meeting, Tyler stood up to the execs. He told them that watering down the script would make the story less powerful. He genuinely believed it would hurt the film. Producers, writers, and directors don't often stand up to the studio, so this brought a smile to my face. A smile that I hid from the execs. Tyler reminded me that there was a "show" part to show business. He wasn't being a roadblock, he was protecting the "show."

But the studio execs were insistent and, finally, forty minutes into the meeting, one of them noticed that the writer, me, was actually in the room. So he asked me what I thought the solution might be. And he didn't mean a compromise. He meant how would I add doubt to the script.

I told him that I could have the doubt come from the other characters, not from the professor. The doubt could be external, not internal to our hero. The doubt could rise up in the world where others would question the authenticity of the video. But the professor would still know that the video was authentic, so the powerful emotional impact of his discovery would stay intact.

The studio execs liked this idea and Tyler politely said that it was "interesting." Then, as if I'd left the room, the execs went on to discuss how this might play out in the script. I took notes and I, myself, wondered how it might play out in the script. I also thought, how odd it was that God and faith weren't part of this discussion about doubt. There was no metaphysical argument in the room.

The meeting ended with the studio getting their way. I was to do a rewrite that added more doubt.

I went back to my cave and I rewrote the script. I came up with an organic solution to creating doubt. The mythical evil creatures, the ones that attack the professor to keep him from revealing God's miracle, destroy the original scroll. So after the professor deciphers the code and shows the video clip of Christ to the world, the world is left without actual proof that this is a true miracle. It all comes down to faith again.

The studio and Tyler liked the rewrite. The studio said they were now going to get a lead actor on board. I was happy with this result. It was another chance at getting a studio film made. The lottery ticket mindset reared her beautiful, seductive head. I tried to chase her away, but I also enjoyed seeing her.

At the same time, I was surprised that none of the studio execs, or Tyler, mentioned what seemed obvious. That the doubt in the outside world ended up undercutting the professor's personal transformation. His emotional epiphany at the end wasn't as powerful as it had been. But I didn't dwell on this flaw. The "business" part of show business was going well. I now had two projects that could easily find their way into theaters.

My career was on the fast track and I was moving closer to meeting my financial goal.

I'm reliving glory days. I'm not using Struggle vs Effort to shine a light on my writing. And, like all the Principles, if I'm not honest with myself, this Principle won't do what I'm asking it to do.

So I gather myself and I accept what I don't want to accept. I can't avoid it. My writing has become more of a struggle. That's what this Principle is telling me. And whether or not that's because I'm stuck down here in my deadworld doesn't matter. What matters is that it's true.

Accepting this doesn't give me the answer to what's missing, but it does move me one step closer to finding that answer.

45

Before I get a chance to apply Struggle vs Effort or the other two new Principles to my list of projects, a pitch that I've been working on moves forward. So I spend more time on it. I'm still spending the bulk of my time writing the script for "Buggs Lake" and I'm also waiting to hear about the network pilot.

This new pitch was propelled up my list by external Energy. I'd been exposing the "one-liner" for this pitch to producers, and I'd been getting good responses, but one producer, on the Warner Brothers lot, the very the heart of the coconut, fell totally in love with it. The "one-liner" captured his imagination. He was sure that the concept would deliver a great film.

The standard definition of a "one-liner" is a sentence or two, which summarizes a script or a pitch. But this definition doesn't get to the heart of what a great one-liner really is and misunderstanding what a one-liner is has killed more nascent screenwriting careers than lack of talent. Here's an example of why, an example that plays out in writers' caves all over town:

A screenwriter spends months or longer writing his screenplay and then he comes up with his one-liner. He needs the one-liner to get agents, producers and execs to read his screenplay. But he quickly discovers that no one is responding to his one-liner and he's sure that there's something wrong with it. So he goes back to the drawing board and spends weeks struggling to make his one-liner sing. But he just can't get it quite right. Why?

Because the vast majority of the time, it's not the one-liner that's the problem, it's the screenplay itself. His screenplay was built on a concept that didn't work or wasn't fresh enough. That was the reason no one responded to his one-liner.

And that's why *Concept is King* when it comes to selling a script or a pitch to a Hollywood studio. Some writers say that "Story is King," but Story becomes King only *after* Concept has relinquished his crown. In a one-liner, Concept still wears the crown. A Hollywood writer sees his one-liner as his concept along with the *promise* of his story.

The Warner Brothers producer was hooked by my one-liner and that meant it had delivered on the concept for my pitch *and* it had promised to deliver a specific story based on that concept. So I work on that story for a few weeks and I go back to the producer and I pitch it to him.

He likes it and he gives me his notes. Then he says that he'd like me to pitch it to this "hot" director who has a deal at Warner Brothers. This is great news. If we can attach this director to the pitch before going into Warner Brothers, then Warner Brothers is more likely to buy the pitch.

The Principles are paying off even better than they did for my old self. I'm very close to three paying jobs, including this job at the very heart of the coconut.

46

Rachel gets that job offer. She tells me over dinner. I still don't want her to take it and we argue about it again. She tells me that she doesn't want to be a stay-at-home mom. It's not who she is. She's not happy. I say she's not happy because Sarah is gone and she calmly says, "And that's not going to change, is it?"

I don't know if she means that she's never going to be happy again or that Sarah is never coming back. And I don't ask her. I go back to the you-need-to-take-care-of-Jake argument, but she says Jake is doing fine. And she's right, so I can't argue that point either. I also can't come up with any new reason for why she shouldn't go back to work. Why should I begrudge her what she wants to do? Why shouldn't her life move forward?

I take a deep breath, drop my combative front, and I ask her what her hours would be at the new job. The argument is over and we both know that there shouldn't have been an argument in the first place. She was always going to take the job, if offered, but she had the courtesy to run it by me, even though it meant putting up with my irrational and bad-tempered resistance.

She tells me that she wants to start out by working two days a week and see how it goes. And now that we're not arguing about it anymore, she lets her excitement shine through. It makes me happy to see her happy.

I implement the Warner Brothers producer's notes and he sets the pitch meeting with the hot director.

We go in and pitch him and he loves it and wants to go into Warner Brothers. He has notes (who doesn't?) and, while I wait for the Warner Brothers meeting to be set, I implement his notes. I also continue to work on "Buggs Lake" and I finally get down to implementing Struggle vs Effort and the other two new Principles.

47

The Principle of Don't Know, Don't Go, was the counterbalance to Al Bernstein's quote, "Sometimes the fool who rushes in gets the job done." It said that if I wasn't sure what to do next, don't do anything... *yet*.

This Principle said that it was okay if I "didn't know." If I wasn't sure what action to take, don't take any. Be patient. But don't wait forever, either. This Principle guarded against impatience, but didn't excuse procrastination.

The Principle of Ride the Wave came into play once I started achieving some of my goals. The momentum and the Energy surrounding my goals became more powerful. I felt like I was riding a giant wave that was sweeping me forward at warp speed. And the more success I had, the more that wave grew.

But I noticed that it grew at an exponential rate, so it got harder to ride at an exponential rate. If I wasn't vigilant about adhering to all the Principles, or if I became overconfident or arrogant, I would tumble off. And I tumbled off many times.

Before the era of Principles, I always rode the wave badly. That wasn't a surprise when I figured out that riding the wave required me to keep my ego in check. And ego is a powerful force. It wants to be recognized as the prime creator of the wave. When things were going my way, ego told me that I was brilliant and talented. It never mentioned that I was the same person whose work had been rejected all over town just a couple of years prior.

I realized that if I took action based on what ego wanted, validation, it was a sure way to tumble off the wave. But if I took action because the Principles dictated it, I'd continue to ride the wave.

I go back into my notebooks and find the section where my old self rode the wave fairly well. Sig Reinfeld, the producer on "The Curse," quickly found a director who wanted to come on board. And not just any director. William Weller had directed a couple of studio films, one of which had been a huge success, and that success was in the same genre as "The Curse." I couldn't have planned for a better fit.

But before committing, Weller wanted to meet me and talk about the script. I'd met with many top directors over the years. These meetings are part of every working writer's routine. A writer is either trying to get a director on board one of his projects, or he's auditioning to write one of the director's projects.

But this meeting wasn't for those reasons. Sig made it perfectly clear that this meeting was to *keep* Weller on board, not to get him on board. Weller already liked the script and considered himself on board. But he wanted to meet me to see if we'd get along and if we had the same "vision" for the film. My job was to make sure that Weller didn't jump ship. If the meeting went well, Sig would then take Weller into Windstorm, who had to approve him, and we could start casting "The Curse."

48

William Weller lived in the Hollywood Hills. That meant that he lived five minutes away from me. But I was anxious about being late, so I planned for L.A. traffic, and I gave myself twenty minutes to get there.

Laurel Canyon was completely traffic free, and two minutes later, I found myself in front of Weller's house, ridiculously early. I parked down the block and waited. I knew the script backward and forward so I didn't have to review it. Instead, I kept repeating to myself that I should listen to whatever Weller had to say and keep my mouth shut. I wasn't a born salesman, but I did know one sales principle. Once a sale was made, it was best to shut-up and make a quick exit.

My script had already made the sale. Weller was on board. So I didn't want to say anything that might cause him to change his mind. On the other hand, I also didn't want to seem morose. It would be a balancing act. Like everything.

I knocked on Weller's front door and his wife

answered. She was beautiful. And not fake Hollywood beautiful, either. But fresh good looks, with a hint of make-up, emerald green eyes that sparkled with life, and natural, golden hair.

She introduced herself as Lily. She looked to be in her late twenties and that meant that she was ten to fifteen years younger than Weller. I immediately jumped to the conclusion that Weller had used his fame and fortune to trick a younger woman, a truly gorgeous woman, into marrying him.

I buried that negative thought. Why would I turn on Weller before I even met him? I'd be falling off the wave when I was literally standing at the threshold of getting "The Curse" made.

Lily invited me in and offered me soda or wine. I asked for water and a little girl, around Sarah's age, came running into the living room. She was blond and all smiles and energy. Lily introduced us and I wanted to say that I, too, have a daughter, but I was afraid that would lead to a series of questions, and that those questions would lead to Sarah's leukemia.

Lily said that her husband would be out in a minute, then she headed to the kitchen. Her daughter, not shy in the least, blurted out that she was getting a cat soon. She quickly qualified that by saying that she *hoped* she'd be getting a cat. It sounded to me like her parents hadn't quite caved in yet.

I told her that cats were the best and that I had a cat, so she wanted to know all about my cat. As I filled her in, I suddenly heard Weller's voice booming out in the background. I could tell that he was on the phone and that he was demanding some kind of perk. I listened to him bully whoever was on the other end of the line while I also listened to his daughter tell me how much she wanted a cat. I pictured their reactions if neither got their way. Weller would be angry and his daughter would be sad. That's because his daughter didn't feel entitled to a cat, but Weller felt entitled to his perk.

Luckily, before that negative thought grew any bigger, Lily returned with my water, and a few seconds later, Weller stepped into the living room.

He was a big guy with a confident stride but, before he even said a word, I sensed that he wanted to wrap this meeting up.

We shook hands, exchanged greetings, and his daughter pointed to me and said, "He says cats are the best thing in the world." Perfect. Now not only was Weller in a hurry to get rid of me, but he also thought that I'd conspired with his daughter to force him to deliver this cat.

Lily and his daughter exited and Weller told me that we could dispense with the small talk. He was waiting for an important call. I gave myself kudos. He *did* want to wrap this up as fast as possible. Probably because he wanted to get back to demanding his perk.

He jumped right in and asked me how I'd come up with the idea for "The Curse." I told him that I was inspired by "Rumpelstiltskin," the fairy tale about a mother who had to give up her first born, and I walked him through the classic version of the fairy tale.

Then I explained how I'd spun it into a modern gothic story that unfolded in a southern city. A city steeped in folklore and superstition. The kind of superstition that a contemporary mother would never believe in. In the script, the mother discovers that her daughter's life was promised as payment for another life saved long ago. But she doesn't believe in this supernatural bargain until her daughter starts to die. Then she begs to substitute her own life as payment, but her life isn't acceptable.

So, like in Rumpelstiltskin, she has to solve the mystery behind that original, supernatural bargain to save her daughter's life.

Weller liked what he was hearing, but I could tell that he wasn't riveted to my tale. He asked a few questions, trying to dig deeper into the script.

I knew what he wanted. He wanted a deeper emotional connection to the story. *And* I had exactly what he wanted.

I knew that if I told him my own story, about Sarah, he would've been riveted and all his questions would've been answered. If I told him that "The Curse" was another direct appeal to God to save my daughter, he would've understood every nuance of the script. If I told him how many times I'd prayed to God to take my life instead of Sarah's, he'd have all the raw emotional material he needed to make my script sing.

Or he might have run away. Just like I was doing by not telling him any of this.

After the questions, Weller segued into the changes he'd liked to see in the script. I reacted positively. That was a no-brainer. If I could move this project forward and Windstorm hired him, we'd be one step closer to production.

As he continued to lay out his notes, I started to

notice something odd. His notes were all over the place, but not all over the place in the usual way, where the person giving the notes hasn't thought everything through. It was more like he was talking about a different film. That was worrisome.

I asked a few questions to let him know that I was tracking exactly what he was saying. But I didn't ask any of the tough questions. The questions that dealt with how his notes would ripple through the script changing every major beat and character arc. This wasn't the time to talk about the heavy-lifting.

After about twenty minutes of notes, Weller started talking about another movie. A foreign film. He said it reminded him of my script and, as he described it in more detail, I realized that his notes came directly from that film. That's why his notes had sounded like he was talking about a different film. He *had* been talking about a different film. And fifteen minutes into talking about this film, I realized something else. He wanted me to lift its plot and insert it into my script.

I was shocked. Not because he wanted me to recycle this plot. Hollywood constantly recycles plots, "recycle" being the Hollywood euphemism for lifting. But I was shocked because he wanted to recycle this plot even though "The Curse" was already set-up. Windstorm already wanted to make the "The Curse." At this point, Weller didn't have to sell anything to anyone. If ain't broke, don't fix it. And, if you don't like the script, don't direct it.

I was ready for notes, but not for this. This could easily turn into a major roadblock.

Weller told me that he'd like me to watch the foreign film and tell him what I thought. I already knew what I thought. I thought this was a page-one rewrite, but I didn't tell him that. (A "page-one" rewrite is when the rewrite of a script entails writing a completely new script.) Instead, I told him that I'd watch the film.

Then the conversation turned to small talk and he started complaining about a film that he'd been in the mix to direct, but didn't get. That film went on to become a huge hit, bigger than his own hit film. Again, I didn't say what I was thinking. I found it absurd that those at the top of the Hollywood totem pole complained about "what might've been" as much as those at the bottom.

While Weller rambled on about how close he'd come to directing that big hit, I thought about a pitch meeting I'd had with a top studio director who'd also complained about missing out on a coveted directing assignment. This was a director who'd had a string of successes and, at the time, was considered one the top three directors in town. He'd wanted me to sympathize with him and he'd been put off when I hadn't. Lesson learned.

This time, I didn't make that mistake. I sympathized with Weller and made sure he could tell.

We wrapped it up and he ushered me to his front door, complimented me on my script, and told me to call him after I watched the foreign film.

On my short drive home, I called Sig, the producer, to report on the meeting. Every meeting in Hollywood is categorized as either "great" or "bad." In Hollywood's entire history, there has never been a meeting that was just "okay." I knew that my meeting hadn't been great. Weller and I hadn't bonded or become blood brothers. And I knew that it hadn't been bad. I was sure that Weller thought we could work together. That left me with only one choice.

I told Sig that the meeting had been "great" and I filled him in on the details, leaving out the part about the foreign film. Sig said he'd check-in with Weller and try to get him into Windstorm as soon as possible.

As I drove down Laurel Canyon, I wondered if Weller might wait until I called him about the foreign film before agreeing to go into Windstorm. He might first want to hear that I'm willing to recycle that plot. And I wondered if Sig knew about Weller's "vision." Did Sig want me to agree to this page-one rewrite? What would Windstorm think? They were writing the checks and they liked the script as is. Would they want to bring on a director who wanted a page-one rewrite?

What actually happened next was the one thing I would've never predicted. But I don't think about that now. Instead, I close my notebook, leave my old self behind, and I concentrate on implementing Struggle vs Effort, Don't Know, Don't Go, and Ride The Wave.

49

As soon as I integrate those Principles into my routine, some of my other projects start to rocket forward. So with "Buggs Lake," the Warner Brothers pitch, and my TV pilot all very much alive, the wave keeps rolling.

I find out that my TV pilot is the only script left standing at the network. The EVP is going to sit down with the rest of the network brass and they'll decide whether to greenlight it or not. That means the network will decide whether to shoot the pilot. Once again, after many, many close calls, I may finally have something produced by a major buyer.

I concentrate on the Principles, implementing them everyday, and I finish the first draft of "Buggs Lake." It's really a fifth draft. I don't like to turn anything in unless it's ready. A script, just like a person, gets only one chance to make a good first impression.

I think the draft is great. It's imbued with an inner life that makes it one of the best things I've ever written. I have no idea why it turned out so well. For some reason, this draft is sprinkled with that magic fairy dust.

Kerry Upland, one of the newer agents on my account, wants to read the draft before I give it to Bill Goode, the producer. Kerry is always hypercritical of my work, but I'm used to it. It's not like my work never gets bashed, that's part of every screenwriter's life, but when he bashes my work, it rubs me the wrong way.

When it comes to giving notes, he can't separate the bad from the almost there. His notes are classic examples of throwing the baby out with the bathwater, and any working screenwriter knows that the vast majority of the time, the only way to improve a script is to dig deeper into what's already there.

But Kerry's notes never do that. His notes are always about the script he would've liked to read rather than the one he actually read. It's always easier to give notes on a story that isn't on paper than to dig deeper into the story that *is* on paper. When I find a producer or an exec who digs deeper into the script or pitch I've given them, I stick with them. "The Curse" and the TV pilot are the results of working with producers who dug deep and helped me find gold.

But if I don't let Kerry read "Buggs Lake," he'll be insulted and he might start to ride the wave badly. That's the more significant consideration. So I tell myself that I don't care how he responds, I know this draft is great, and I email him the script and wait for his harsh criticism.

On Monday morning, I get to my office, and go through my morning routine. It's now longer because I've integrated almost all the Principles into it. Then, before I start writing, I reach over to shut off my phone, but it rings.

I can see from the number that it's my agency. That means it's one of my agents. I'm sure it's Kerry and I'm sure he read the script over the weekend.

I brace myself for the battle over his notes.

50

I pick up the phone and Kerry tells me that it's the best script I've ever written. He says he's proud of me. I'm stunned and I literally don't know how to respond.

He goes on with his praise until I finally say, thanks. He does have some notes, but he says that I should send the draft to Bill and get his input first.

I email the script to Bill and I wonder if Kerry has turned over a new leaf. I hope he likes the script enough to help push it all the way into production.

Three days later, Bill calls me and tells me he loves the script. He can't believe it's only a first draft. Of course, he does have notes and this makes me nervous, until he tells me what they are. I'm elated. His notes are great. They dig deeper into the script and are totally organic to the story.

I implement his notes right away and, a week later, I give him another read. He signs off and I turn "Buggs Lake" into the production company.

The next Monday, the president of the production

company calls me and tells me that he loves the script. I'm happy to hear that because I truly believe this is a good script and I would've been disappointed if he hadn't agreed.

At the end of the call, he says that he wants to set a meeting to discuss the next step. Since he likes the script, my guess is that the next step will be getting a director or an actor on board. The wave keeps rolling.

51

I was wrong about Rachel's job. She seems happier than she's been in a long time and she has plenty of time for Jake.

I don't ask her if she's actually happy, rather than happier. Right after Sarah died, she had told me that she didn't think she could ever be happy again. If I heard her say that again, I'd give up trying to climb out of my deadworld. What would be the point if she wasn't happy? So instead of asking her if she's happy, I accept that she's happi*er* and I let it go at that.

One weekend afternoon, Rachel and I go out for a hike in Fryman Canyon. It rained the day before, so when we reach the top of the trail, we can see the entire eastern part of the Valley. It's a sparkling, expansive tableau of greens and browns and perfect geometric shapes, and in the distance, the grand San Gabriel Mountains tower over it all like ancient guards on watch.

From up here, it looks like the L.A. of the fifties, clean, clear, with unlimited opportunity for all. Everybody had a shot at fulfilling his or her dreams.

Rachel brings up my recent successes and she says she knew I'd recover. She knew that I'd learn to live with the hole in my heart. Tears come to her eyes, tears for Sarah.

Whenever we talk about Sarah, she cries. I don't want her to cry, but I know she can't help it. And why shouldn't she cry? So I do the usual. I change the subject.

I talk about Jake. He's adjusting and I'm proud of him. He's doing well in school and he doesn't appear to be depressed. The only weird thing is that his close group of friends, the ones he's known since birth, the ones who also grew up with Sarah, have been picking on him. I have no idea why and it makes me angry. Why would his best friends turn on him when he needs them the most?

Rachel tells me why. She explains that not only does Jake have to process Sarah's death, but so do Sarah's friends. And Sarah's friends are Jake's friends. They're picking on him because he reminds them that Sarah died. He reminds them that one of their best friends is never coming back. He reminds them that life is fleeting, that they can die at six. A harsh truth that no six-year-old should have to face.

I feel ashamed of my anger.

As for Jake, he's not the least bit angry at his friends. He's social and outgoing, so getting picked on doesn't stop him from wanting to be with his friends. He cries and he asks us why they're being mean to him, but then he completely forgets about it and wants to play with them again. He has a good attitude. Way better than mine. He doesn't hold a grudge. At all.

That's a great principle to follow.

52

A couple of days after hearing the good news on "Buggs Lake," I hear more good news. The meeting for the Warner Brothers' pitch is set. This pitch is a textbook case of following the Principle of The Path of Least Resistance. I never had a pitch move forward so quickly into a studio.

But this success still doesn't feel as good as it would've in the past, and I'm tempted to analyze why, but I don't. Instead, I dive back into my notebooks to extract more of the Principles.

I see that I was fast approaching my financial goal. And this was also the time when Sarah's chemo treatments were coming to an end. She'd responded well to the treatments, she was in remission, and her odds of survival were now even greater. Her last treatment was going to be in June so we'd planned a joyous summer.

I didn't want to do too much that summer. I thought if we overdid it, Sarah might relapse. A doctor had told us that contracting leukemia was horrible, but whatever you do, don't get it twice. His gallows humor had turned Rachel and me off (we never went back to him for advice), but I never forgot his blunt decree. After a relapse, the survival rate was tiny. Relapse was our greatest fear.

Rachel wanted to do more that summer than I did. She wanted Sarah to enjoy life. I thought Sarah would have plenty of time to enjoy life after we made sure that she didn't relapse. I got my way, which I now regret. We were conservative and, looking back, I wish we'd done a hell of a lot more. At least, Rachel pushed to spend a lot of time at the beach and I'm grateful for that. Sarah loved the beach.

That summer, after Sarah's treatments ended, we headed to the wide golden beaches of Venice and Zuma. Sarah was a good swimmer and she bobbed up and down in the blue Pacific for hours. Afterward, in the cool evening breeze, we'd ride bikes along the beachfront bike path, stopping to play in the playgrounds along the way. We were like a normal family.

I don't want to relive what happened next. I don't want to relive the nightmare that buried me in my deadworld. So I focus on exactly what's written down in my notebooks. I focus on the glory days, reaching my financial goal, and I don't read between the lines, where the pain is hidden.

I see that I still hadn't heard from Sig Rienfeld, the producer on "The Curse," and that meant he still hadn't heard from William Weller, the director. So I decided that I'd better watch that foreign film and call

Weller.

I tracked the film down and I watched it. It was nothing like "The Curse." The plot, the setting, and the characters were nothing like my script. The only similarity was the tone. That's what Weller must've have tuned into, and that's what must've given him the brilliant idea of recycling its plot. If Windstorm approved Weller as director, and went along with his plan, I'd be launched into a page-one rewrite. And a major rewrite always leads to a major roadblock.

But, for right now, my job was to keep this project moving forward. And that meant keeping Weller on board. So I called him and I told him that I loved the foreign film, which wasn't a lie. I *did* love the film. Then I told him that I had a few ideas about how to implement his notes. This wasn't a lie either. I *did* have a few ideas. But I didn't tell him that they didn't involve recycling the plot.

We chatted about the film and then he told me that he looked forward to hearing what I'd come up with. After I hung up, I hoped that he'd immediately call Sig and tell him that we were on the same page, and that, in turn, Sig would bring him into Windstorm.

I was riding the wave and it was moving fast. The day after I called Weller, I suddenly got another job. I was hired for a production rewrite on a project that I'd sold years ago.

A production rewrite is a rewrite on a film that's already been greenlit. If a writer lands a production rewrite and that film goes on to do well at the box office, then that writer is in the production rewrite business. This pays better than any other writing job in Hollywood. I calculated that in the eighth week of the rewrite, if it went that long, I'd receive the paycheck that would put me over my financial goal.

53

The studio that owned this old project wanted to put it into production because Rice Cooper, an A-level director, wanted to make it. The studio had bought my script almost a decade ago and I'd rewritten it for them a number of times. But I was eventually booted off and replaced. That led to three years of rewrites by four other writers until the studio let the project die.

It stayed dead for five years until one of the original drafts made it into the hands of Rice Cooper and he took a liking to it. When an A-level director agrees to board a script, it's like he or she gives the script mouth-to-mouth resuscitation and brings it back to life.

Rice Cooper didn't live in L.A., so the studio rented him a bungalow in the Pacific Palisades, and that's where I started working with him. He was an older director and, like most directors who've had long careers, he'd had both hits and misses. But his hits included two iconic films and those films guaranteed that he'd always find work.

As I worked with him, I learned that he was a real cinephile. He'd seen huge swathes of films from the thirties, forties, and fifties. Films from Hollywood's Golden Age. And not only had he seen them, he'd also studied how they worked and why. Rice Cooper helped turn my script into a real gem and, after four weeks, he gave the draft to the studio. He told them that this was the film he wanted to make.

The studio liked the draft, but they didn't give Rice the go-ahead to move into production. Instead, they continued to pay us both as we waited for the official word.

A few weeks passed and Rice started to get upset. He wanted the studio to make a "goddamn decision." He didn't want to wait around, collecting his paychecks, while the studio twiddled its thumbs. He'd been putting together an independent film and he was ready to leave L.A. and get back to it. Rice was a filmmaker first and he'd rather be making a film, even a small, independent film, than waiting on a studio.

While we were waiting, I received the paycheck that put me over the top. I reached my financial goal and I thanked the Principles for working their magic. Their magic was so powerful that the paycheck that put me over the top, was handed to me for literally doing nothing.

At this point, the memory that I don't want to think about is unavoidable. It's the memory of what happened right on the heels of this triumph. It's the part of my life where the Principles don't work their magic. It's a long, vivid memory that always ends in heartbreak.

54

That summer ended and it was a time of celebration, both professionally and personally. I'd met my goal and Sarah had made it through the summer, leukemia free. There'd be no more chemo and no more suffering.

That Monday, Labor Day weekend, was my birthday and we drove out to Paradise Cove, a small, pristine beach in Malibu. We spent the day on the warm, golden sand, and Sarah and Jake swam in the cold Pacific, racing each other out to sea and back. We built villages in the sand and we watched the waves tear them down.

Then, in the orange glow of the setting sun, we celebrated my birthday with dinner at the Paradise Cove restaurant. We told each other crazy jokes about sharks and whales and their adventures and we laughed and laughed. I thought I was the luckiest guy in the world. Sarah had survived leukemia and I now had two healthy, happy kids, a beautiful, smart wife, and my career was going better than I'd ever imagined.

Four days later, my luck ran out.

55

Labor Day weekend ended and Sarah and Jake started kindergarten. Sarah loved it. She'd missed most of pre-K and she barely remembered the normalcy of nursery school. Kindergarten was her chance to be a normal kid again and she was savoring every second of it.

On the morning of the fourth day, Rachel and I walked Sarah and Jake to school. I watched Sarah run into her classroom to join her new friends. She was laughing before she even reached them. I was as happy as she was.

That afternoon, Rachel took Sarah and Jake to the hospital for Sarah's monthly check-up and I headed to the Paramount lot to meet with a production company. This company financed their own films and they were interested in a spec I'd written. I had high hopes for the meeting. The Principles had delivered on my financial goal, so I had set a new goal. Getting a film into production. And this company had said it might buy my spec and go directly into production.

So, as I drove through the Paramount gates, I was

thinking that this could be the fastest that I'd ever reached any of my goals.

As soon as I parked on the lot, my cell phone rang. I saw it was Rachel and picked up. She immediately asked me what I was doing. I said I was about to walk into a meeting and she asked me to call her back afterward.

I knew something was wrong. I could hear it in her voice. I asked her, what was up, and she said, "Nothing, we'll talk later." But I was so pumped up for this meeting, that I insisted she tell me. She relented.

She told me that Sarah had relapsed.

I went numb.

Then I felt dread flooding through my body and pooling in my soul. This couldn't be happening. It was all starting again. Random tragedy had been thrown at Sarah. An innocent six-year-old. What happened to Paradise Cove?

Rachel was crying on the other end of the line and I told her that I'd meet her at the hospital. She said, no, go to your meeting, you can't cancel now. You're sitting in the lot.

I hung up and I headed to that meeting. I was indoctrinated by the Principles. Control My Thoughts. Focus On My Goals. Ignore Emotional Distractions.

But, though the Principles pushed me to that meeting, they didn't control my thoughts. As I crossed the Paramount lot, the words of that doctor ran through my head, *It's horrible getting leukemia, but whatever you do, don't get it twice.*

Sarah was going to die.

56

I sat in that meeting, listening to the production company's top exec, an alpha male, going through his notes on my spec.

My spec was about an elite college fraternity whose members were secretly ghosts. They were the kings of the campus, the best athletes, the best students, and they threw the best parties. All the freshmen wanted to rush their frat, but what the freshmen didn't know was that during the hazing rituals, they were slowly dying and becoming ghosts.

The exec, himself, could've easily passed for a member of this elite frat. He was confident and aggressive as he laid out the rules of how ghosts should operate in the world of the living. His rules were different than the ones I'd laid out in my spec. But because I'd just learned that Sarah was going to die, his rules didn't sound just "different," they sounded like arrogant pontificating. This exec was *the* expert on death. He knew how the dead operated in the world of the living. Didn't he understand that "nobody knows anything?" Especially about death. My daughter was going to die and here he was telling me he knew what was going to happen to her afterward.

But it wasn't his fault that he sounded like a bloviating fool. It was my fault. I should've canceled the meeting. Instead, I sat there listening to his rules and I thought about Sarah. If she died would she return as a ghost? I crushed that thought. She wasn't going to die. I needed to get the hell out of there and find out what was next. Whatever it was, I knew it would involve vicious and painful treatments for Sarah. I felt awful for her.

I also knew that there'd be the option of doing nothing. It'd been an option the first time around. I'd looked into doing nothing as well as doing "natural" treatments. Rachel had been a hundred percent against either of those options. I'd done the research and made my case to her, but I, myself, hadn't been convinced. If we had opted to do nothing or "natural" treatments and Sarah had died, I would've always blamed myself for not giving her the best that modern medicine could offer. But now modern medicine had failed us.

I told the exec that I would change the rules about ghosts. I wanted to get the hell out of there. He then went on to his other notes.

I listened, but I was thinking about going to the hospital and asking the doctors hundreds of question. I was also wondering if Rachel had told Sarah. Did Sarah know that bad luck had tracked her down again?

Finally, the exec finished with his notes and asked me if I had any questions. I wanted to say, yes, hundreds of them, but they're all about my daughter and I don't think you can answer any of them.

I said, "No, not right now," and I ran out of there.

57

After one summer of feeling like a normal family, we went back to fighting our archenemy, leukemia. We went back to defending and protecting Sarah. Back to chemo treatments and Sarah in pain.

I told Sarah that everything would be fine. But that was the biggest lie I'd ever told. And I was sure that she was picking up on it. But I couldn't tell her that the odds of her surviving were awful.

I tried to focus on the miracles. On the people who'd survived a relapse. I found every example I could, but the sobering reality was that there weren't that many. And what made it worse, was that when I dug deep into those few miracles, miracles that matched Sarah's exact diagnosis, they were all questionable.

The memories from this time are vivid, but they're not written down in my notebooks. Instead, they silently cling to what I find on the pages. I see that it became harder to focus on work, though I still needed to. Especially if I wanted to ride the wave. I was still waiting on Sig Reinfeld, the producer of "The Curse," to call me. I'd had my phone call with Weller, where I'd told him how much I loved the foreign film, but I hadn't heard a word from him or from Sig.

I weighed whether to call Weller to see if he wanted to get together and talk about implementing his notes. Maybe everyone was waiting on me. Maybe the only way to keep Weller on board was to rewrite the script according to his notes.

The Principles weren't leading me in any one direction about what do to. That was probably because I was spending less time on the Principles and more time in my own private Idaho of Sarah's relapse. I was learning about bone marrow transplants, the only real option for her. The transplant was a long process that involved more chemo treatments and Sarah would have to go into remission first. But without a bone marrow transplant, she'd die. One hundred percent.

Sarah would also need a bone marrow donor and we'd already started that search. There was a national bank of donors and Rachel, Jake and I were also tested.

Finally, Sig called me. By then, I was thinking one of two things. Either Sig had already taken Weller into Windstorm and we were ready to make the film, or Weller wanted the script changed first. But Sig told me the one thing I least expected. Windstorm wasn't interested in meeting with Weller. At all. I couldn't believe it. Getting Weller was a coup.

Sig was furious. He told me that he'd spent months explaining to Windstorm that Weller was the perfect fit for "The Curse." That's what had been taking so long.

As he vented, I got a bad feeling. Sig was souring on the project. He'd delivered an A-level director and this was his reward. Windstorm's rejection was a personal affront to him.

And, Sig had put his own reputation on the line with Weller. He had told Weller that Windstorm wanted him on board and it was a done deal. Now he was going to have to tell him that Windstorm didn't even want to meet with him. Who the hell did Windstorm think they were?

When I hung up, I knew that Sig Reinfeld wasn't going to deliver another director. I'd been lucky to have Sig's attention and I knew I wouldn't have it again for a while, if at all.

This felt like a turn in momentum. Like I might be falling off the wave.

58

I scrutinize the notebooks to see exactly what happened next. The Principles were definitely fading. With every passing week, I was applying them less. Sarah was more important than the Principles. The reality of life was right there in front of me, and I couldn't control it.

In my notebooks, I also see that my list of projects was frozen in place. If I'd been applying the Principles more often, my focus would've smoothly shifted from one project to the next, reading their Energy, and moving them up and down my list.

The fall of "The Curse" should've sent it sliding down my list, but it's still right up there, just under my production rewrite. I was still waiting for a real greenlight on the rewrite and I'd collected another few paychecks for doing nothing. I hadn't spoken to Rice Cooper, the director, for a few weeks.

But one evening, Rice called and told me that he'd had it. He wasn't waiting any longer. He was ready to confront the studio. If the studio didn't agree to go into production, he'd give up the free paychecks, leave L.A., and go back to his independent film.

His agents were telling him to be patient. They wanted him to wait it out a little longer. They were collecting free paychecks, too. But Rice didn't care what his agents wanted. He went ahead and set a meeting with the studio.

I agreed with his agents. Not only because of the free paychecks, but also because of my new goal. To get a film into production. I thought confronting the studio would jeopardize that goal. If Rice put the studio on the spot, they might pull the plug.

But I kept my opinion to myself and let Rice vent. This was his baby. He had breathed life into it, and if he killed it, that seemed like the proper way for it to die. And, this denouement would fit perfectly with the change of momentum I was feeling.

Rice went in for the meeting and called me afterward. He got right to the point. The studio had pulled the plug. The film was dead and he was heading home.

I had fallen off the wave.

But, on the heals of this, I received great news. News that dwarfed falling off the wave. Sarah was in remission. Unfortunately, this was tempered by the next front in the battle for Sarah's life. The bone marrow transplant.

First came the decision on who'd be the donor. Rachel and I weren't a match. It turned out that there were varying degrees of matches, based on antigen markers. The best match was six out of six. Rachel and I were both four out of six. The donor list had yielded a match of five out of six, which was good, but not ideal.

One person was an ideal match. Jake. Six out of six. A perfect match. But I didn't want to risk Jake's life.

The transplant specialist assured us that Jake wouldn't be at risk. He said that it was a routine operation. Rachel was ready to move forward. I wanted to continue looking for another donor.

The problem with my strategy was that the longer we waited, the more we were risking Sarah's life. The leukemia could return any day and, if it did, the hospital wouldn't allow her to have the transplant. Her only hope at life, slim as it was, would be gone.

Rachel was sure that Jake would be safe and I feared losing both my kids. The doctors told me that my fear was understandable, but irrational. I knew my fear was irrational. I couldn't find one example of a bone marrow donor dying from the operation. So I ignored my fear and focused on my hope. My greatest hope. Saving Sarah.

But once I'd fully accepted that Jake would be the donor, I came up with a new worry. I had discovered it when I was researching bone marrow donors. It was called "Survivor's Guilt." If Sarah didn't survive, Jake would feel like a failure. And this worry wasn't an irrational fear. It'd been documented, named, and codified. Even though Jake was a brave six-year-old, trying to save his sister, if Sarah didn't make it, he'd feel like a failure for the rest of his life.

59

The night before the transplant, Sarah was scared. Rachel tried to sooth her, tried to help her fall asleep, but Sarah was too upset. She wasn't upset about the operation. She'd been through hell already. She was upset about what was to follow. Three months in the bone marrow unit, if not longer, isolated from everyone. Sarah thought she might never return to her cozy bedroom.

After three hours of assuring her that everything would be okay, Rachel, frustrated, asked me to take over.

Rachel was scared, too. This had been a long, hard road, full of setbacks, and starting tomorrow, it was going to get a lot harder.

I tried to rock Sarah to sleep. After thirty minutes, she said, "Look at me, dad," and I realized that I'd been avoiding looking at her. I was scared, too.

Jake, who was asleep, was the only one in the house who wasn't scared. We had managed to hide from him that the operation was tomorrow. We had also kept it hidden from Sarah, but I'd let it slip out just after Jake fell asleep. This whole tense night was my fault.

I said to Sarah, you're ready, honey, you're going to be okay, and she said to me, with the weight of the world on her shoulders, I don't want to leave home again, dad. Can't I just stay home?

I tried not to cry. I smiled and repeated that everything was going to be okay. Her eyes betrayed fear and so did mine. She finally fell asleep at three a.m., exhausted.

We rose at dawn and drove to the City of Hope, the hospital with the fitting name. At this stage in Sarah's battle, the only thing we had left was hope.

The car trip was silent. As we approached the City of Hope, Sarah asked us if she had to do this. I wanted to say that she didn't. Maybe we could enjoy life and hope for a miracle. We were basically asking for a miracle anyway.

Rachel assured Sarah that everything would be okay, but fear hung in the air.

Jake and I headed into the hospital and Rachel and Sarah headed to the bone marrow unit.

In the cold, pre-op room, I watched a nurse prep Jake for the operation. A few minutes later, the anesthesiologist stepped in and discussed "going under."

I worried about Jake going under. It was the biggest risk in the operation. After I got over my irrational fear, it remained the one reason I continued to hope for another donor. But it was too late now. Jake was going under. Hopefully, he'd come back. And come back healthy.

Sarah didn't have to go under. But she'd gone under plenty of times in her young life. Before she even contracted leukemia, she'd gone under. At two years old, she'd undergone surgery for an inguinal hernia. I still wonder if that's how she'd contracted leukemia. That operation is one of the suspects in this violent crime. Cutting open Sarah's tiny body at that young age seemed unholy.

The doctor performing the transplant walked into the pre-op room and started explaining the procedure. He explained it to me and ignored Jake. Jake listened intently anyway.

When the doctor wrapped it up and asked me if I had any questions, Jake chimed in. *He* had questions. The doctor was surprised. But what surprised him even more was that Jake's questions were all legitimate. How many times had the doctor performed this kind of operation? Had he ever made a puncture in the wrong place? Was there ever a problem with the depth of the puncture? How did the doctor know when he'd collected enough bone marrow?

The doctor answered each of Jake's questions and Jake appeared to be satisfied. A few minutes later, the nurse came in to wheel Jake out.

I told Jake that everything was going to be okay, that he was a brave boy, and that I loved him. Then I watched the nurse wheel him into the operating room. I buried my anxiety deep inside and I headed to the bone marrow unit.

Rachel and Sarah were settling into their room.

Rachel had already driven out a number of times to decorate Sarah's room and to make it as cozy as possible. Sarah's snow globes lined the windowsill, her stuffed kitties lounged on the easy chair, and her lava lamp glowed purple on the night table.

Now that she was here, Sarah was more relaxed. She was a battle-hardened warrior and she was ready for the newest front. At least, this front would start out with a fairly simple procedure. Sarah would receive Jake's bone marrow through an intravenous drip, similar to a blood transfusion. She's had dozens of blood transfusions, so this wouldn't be upsetting. What would be upsetting were the painful treatments required to get the bone marrow to graft.

After an hour, I left the bone marrow unit and stationed myself in the waiting room. A few minutes later, the doctor appeared and told me everything had gone well. Jake was fine. He'd be waking up from the anesthesia in fifteen minutes.

I headed over to the post-op room and I sat by Jake's side until he woke up. He was groggy and confused and spoke haltingly. I was worried.

We talked and I anxiously hoped for him to return to his energetic and overly inquisitive self.

Ten minutes later, he did. He was chattering away and asking me questions that I couldn't answer. He had survived intact. So far. Then he stopped chattering, looked me in the eye and said, "I saved Sarah."

60

My notebooks become more spare from this point on. The memories are still vivid, but I try to focus on what I'm reading on the pages in front of me. I'm sure there's a lesson to be learned here.

I see that I still hadn't changed my list of projects. The list was an ancient, decaying fossil. No longer a living record of my career. And it's hard to tell how intensely I was implementing The Principles or if I was implementing them at all.

It was a long drive out to the City of Hope. Jake and I visited Rachel and Sarah in the bone marrow unit once during the week and every Saturday and Sunday.

During the week, I wrote in my cave and Jake went to school. Jake spent a lot of time in afterschool programs and on playdates with friends. At night, Jake and I ate dinner together, then I'd get him ready for bed and read to him. The house was lonely. We were a family of two sticking it out until the rest of the family returned.

Jake would ask me hundreds of questions. About science, about books he'd read, about math, about current events. But the most important questions were about life. He was six and he was beginning to understand in a more profound way what it meant that Sarah had leukemia. He wanted to know why some kids got it and some didn't.

I told him it was random, but he was way too logical to accept that. He wanted a better explanation. A scientific explanation. I filled him on the theories about viruses and genetic mutations, but I didn't mention my own list of villains.

Sarah had accepted that it was random. She had accepted that it was bad luck. She had grown past looking for villains. She'd once found a penny on the sidewalk, picked it up, and said, "Look, dad, it's a lucky penny," her eyes sparkling. But then she'd immediately added, with a gravitas way beyond her years, "But I'm not lucky, Dad."

I had lied and said, "You *are* lucky," and I'd listed the things she loved as proof. Her mom, her brother, her best friend, Emma, Halloween, blue-raspberry sherbert, and "My Time-Traveling Brother." I don't think she bought it, but she humored me with her big smile.

One night, after reading to Jake, he threw me one of his tough questions, "Does Mom love Sarah more than me?"

My heart broke. I told him, "No," and I explained that Sarah needed her mom more than he did. If he were sick, wouldn't he want to be with his mom?

He said, "Yes," but he wasn't convinced.

Then he asked me the toughest question yet. Did I love him better than Sarah? I immediately said, "Yes," no hesitation at all. I felt guilty about my answer, but instinctually I knew that this was the right answer. I didn't hesitate because I didn't want him to have any doubt. I was sure he believed that his mom loved his sister more, so I wanted him to believe that I loved him more. He'd never once complained about not having his mom around and this was the smallest of rewards for that. The love of the inferior parent.

61

I move forward in my notebooks and I come across the last of my projects from my triumphant period, the only one still moving forward. "The Secret of the Cross."

Tyler Gaverness, the producer on the project, called to tell me that the studio wanted the script rewritten. They'd suddenly decided that my first rewrite didn't work as well as they'd originally thought. Tyler said that the studio had decided that the doubt I'd inserted into the script *did* undercut the professor's epiphany after all.

I had a hard time believing the studio suddenly discovered this kink. I told Tyler that my bet was the studio had sent the script to some of the actors on their list and that those actors had passed, so the studio got cold feet. He said that was possible, but it didn't matter. To keep the project alive, I needed to do the rewrite. Then, he laid out the studio's notes.

As he went through them, I wondered why we weren't going in to meet with the studio to get these notes firsthand. But as the notes piled up, that question faded, and my disappointment grew. This was a page-one rewrite. The studio wanted to rip the heart out of the story.

I asked questions to clarify the notes and I tried not to act defensive. I told myself that I was getting paid for the rewrite and I'd find a way to turn this new draft into a great script. I'd transplant a new heart into the story.

After I hung up with Tyler, I called Ben, my agent, to fill him in on this new roadblock. I told him what I suspected, that a few actors had passed on the script, and he told me that I was right, but only partially. It turned out that the studio had sent the script to one actor and he'd passed.

Now I was angry. One guy had problems with the script and now the studio wanted a page-one rewrite? *And* what made this worse was that Ben didn't know if this actor had actually read the script. It could've been one of his "people."

A couple of days later, I found out that this wasn't what made this worse. What made this worse was that the studio wasn't paying for the rewrite. Officially, they weren't even asking for a rewrite. Tyler Graverness, the producer, was. That was why there'd been no studio meeting about the notes. Officially, a studio can't ask for a free rewrite.

Ben and Tyler wanted me to start on the rewrite immediately. They wanted to keep the momentum going. They were transferring the roadblock designation from the studio to me. That's exactly how the modern studio system works. If a writer doesn't want to work for free, he's the roadblock.

If I'd been applying the Principles and thinking

more positively, I could've easily made an argument for jumping right into the rewrite. I could've convinced myself that those paychecks that I'd received on the production rewrite, paychecks for doing nothing, were the paychecks for doing *this* rewrite. It was all part of the "positive conspiracy" to get me paid. But my downward momentum was gaining so much speed that it was hard to see anything positive. When you're tumbling off the wave, you don't see the blue sky up above. You see the black ocean floor down below.

A week later, I did get some great news. Sarah was cleared to come home from the bone marrow unit and, a few days later, our family was complete again.

But we had a very delicate home life. Sarah wasn't allowed to leave the house. She couldn't be exposed to viruses or germs or anything that might cause infections. An infection could kill her. Still, she was ecstatic to be home and Jake was happy to have his mom and sister back. But Rachel and I were anxious all the time. We wanted this to be a lasting cure. We didn't want the leukemia to return and kill our daughter. The odds were overwhelmingly against us.

Sarah was fine for a couple of months and then Rachel took her in for one of her regular check-ups and the bad news came a couple hours later. The leukemia was back. We both knew that Sarah wasn't going to recover this time. The bone marrow transplant had been nothing but a temporary reprieve.

Rachel and I had already decided what we'd do if Sarah relapsed again. Minimal treatments. Let her live. Let her finally go to school. Let her enjoy what was left of her life. This time, she wouldn't spend months in the hospital, suffering.

The doctors suggested another bone marrow transplant and, of course, even though we'd made our decision, we couldn't reject this out of hand. But we didn't have to consider it until, or if, Sarah went into remission again. And there was no guarantee that she would. This time, we really were counting on a miracle. It was the only cure left.

The next phase of Sarah's life was the good life. She enjoyed school and she had a great time playing with Jake and Emma and with new friends. She loved sleeping in her own bed every night and she loved going to birthday parties and holiday parties. And even though she was getting very low doses of chemotherapy, the leukemia was receding.

The good times lasted four months. Then Sarah came down with an infection, a bad infection, and Rachel rushed her to the City of Hope. The doctors treated her infection, but the treatment went badly off-course. Twenty-four hours later, Sarah died.

I don't want to live through her death again.

62

I close my notebooks and I think about the lessons I learned from watching my old self tumble off the wave. I have to keep implementing the Principles. Seeing how quickly those past projects died is a sobering reminder. I can't let my current list of projects freeze in place. I have to move them forward. Always.

But I also have to admit another truth to myself. One that's far less of a guidepost: I can't tell from the notebooks which came first, abandoning the Principles or the death of my projects.

I *can* say that the Principles did lead me out of that past rough patch. They lead me to my big year. *And* I can say that they're working their magic right now. So it's reasonable to conclude that I have to keep implementing them.

But I can't ignore the bigger picture. I can't ignore the difference between my old self and my new self. Something is missing from my writing this time around. Getting my career back on track isn't enough this time around.

So once more, I tell myself that I'm going to

implement all the Principles and see if that's the key to finding what's missing. I dive into my notebooks, into the sections before I abandoned the Principles, and I pull out the last three.

Let Life Unfold, Favor Yes Over No, and Don't Push Things Away. These three Principles are refinements of the ones I'm already implementing, so it's easy to add them to my routine.

Within a week, they're fully integrated, and then, a week later, they're reinforced with an unforgettable lesson.

I see Ben, my agent, at the after-party for a premiere and he tells me how happy he is that things are going well for me. His statement is a gracious acknowledgement that my hard work has paid off. I thank him for his help.

Then he tells me that he's been using a new business strategy over the past year. He's been saying "no" as much as possible.

What?! I can't believe it. His new strategy is the polar opposite of favoring "yes" over "no." And, as I stand there, covering up my incredulity, and wondering if that's why he's generated fewer meetings for me this year, he goes on to explain his strategy.

He's been rejecting as much of what comes his way as possible. He doesn't return the calls of lower-level producers who fill up his call sheets looking for ways to move their projects past roadblocks. So Ben is also inverting Don't Push Things Away, and, when he says that letting these people into his life means giving up control of his life, I realize that he's completed the trifecta. He's defying Let Life Unfold. He's inverted all three new Principles.

I want to tell him that he should be more open to new people and new projects. I want to tell him that sometimes life has a way of delivering something to your door, something you might want or need, but if you don't answer the door, you'll never know it's been delivered.

But I don't say anything. I can't change him, I can only change myself. Instead, I smile and listen as he continues to lay out his new business strategy.

Two weeks later, Ben gets fired. I take this as a lesson. An unforgettable lesson. Don't invert the Principles.

63

I'm now implementing all the Principles. Every morning, I come into my office and I focus on them, and on my list of projects. Then I get down to writing. I don't want to slack off and end up in the same downward spiral that I saw in my notebooks.

One morning, before I start my routine, the phone rings. I don't pick it up and I don't look at the incoming number. I don't want to be tempted into answering. I don't want to be drawn into an emotional maelstrom that could throw off my writing for the rest of the day.

The phone stops ringing. Good. I shut it off. Then I reach for my cell to shut it off too, but it starts ringing and I can't help but glance at number. It's Gary Rivers, the producer on my TV pilot. I have to pick it up. It might be news about the pilot, about the greenlight.

I pick it up and I can tell from Gary's tone that he's going to deliver bad news. He starts out by telling me that the EVP finally heard back from the network brass. They thought the pilot was a fresh take on a genre that's worked well for the network. They said that I'd created original characters that hadn't yet been explored within this genre. They also said that it was the best pilot script of their development season.

I like the compliments, but I'm bracing for the bad news. I'm hoping that it's not as bad as these compliments might indicate. Maybe the network wants another rewrite. Or maybe the network wants to bring on another writer. But before I can come up with another bad news scenario that's not so bad, Gary delivers the real bad news, which *is* bad. The network isn't going to move forward with the pilot. It's dead.

The Principles are coursing through me and I think that, maybe, this isn't a total downer. Maybe Gary had passed on the network's compliments because they'd decided to save the pilot for next year's pilot season. That's not the case. Gary assures me that the pilot is dead. Completely dead. The network brass felt like it didn't fit in with their long-term vision for the network.

Gary and I chat a little longer. He's trying to cushion the blow, but I've learned to take rejection without much lamenting. The business is about collecting "no's." Edward Vanvich, a director whom I worked with early in my career, gave me some advice that helped me weather the cascade of "no's" that is a screenwriting career.

Vanvich directed a high-profile Hollywood failure and, afterward, was ostracized and rejected by everyone in town. After many years of rejection, he recovered and went on to win an Academy Award. He told me that for every "yes" a writer or director collects, he has to collect nine hundred ninety-nine "no's." So I quickly got used to collecting "no's," building up to that one "yes," and that's the first piece of advice I give to new screenwriters. If you can't take massive and persistent rejection, Hollywood isn't the place for you. Rejection is the rule, not the exception.

The conversation winds down and Gary tells me that he still loves the script. He says that it's a great pilot and he thanks me for all my work.

I thank him for his input and it's a sincere thanks. He carefully poured over every draft and he gave me thoughtful notes. His notes were always organic to the script, always digging deeper. Gary also pushed hard for the project every step of the way. I hang up and I know I'll work with him again.

I start to write, but the disappointment gets in the way. Regardless of the nine hundred ninety-nine rejections philosophy, I have to admit that this is a setback. Sure, I'm back on track and this time around my projects moved forward more easily, but in the end, it's the same old story. No breakthrough to production. And, with the pilot dead, I can't help but wonder if the tide is turning.

I can't abandon the Principles.

I go back to writing and within a few minutes something weird happens. My disappointment fades. Much faster than it ever did in the past. And what's even weirder is that I don't feel too badly about the change in momentum either. I'm sure that's because I'm not going to abandon the Principles this time around. I'm too close to finding out what's missing in my writing and in my life.

64

The next week, Bill Goode and I finally have the meeting with the production company that bought "Buggs Lake." I'd been looking forward to this meeting. They loved the script and I hoped it was headed toward production.

The president of the company and his top development exec start off by apologizing for taking so long to set the meeting. I don't mind. As far as I'm concerned, the timing is perfect. The TV pilot is dead and it's time to focus on getting "Buggs Lake" into production.

The president praises my script again, and I'm embarrassed. It's easier for me to take compliments over the phone. In person, I feel self-conscious and unworthy. I'm ready for him to move on and I expect that after he stops professing his love for the script, he'll feel comfortable bringing up any minor notes he might have. My guess is that he'll ask me to implement those notes for free before he goes out to a director or an actor.

Of course, I'll agree. I want to keep the momentum going.

When he finally stops praising the script, his exec walks over to a table and picks up a stack of papers. I'm surprised. I'm sure it's a stack of notes. If it were a list of directors or actors, it wouldn't be a stack.

The exec hands me a thick set of stabled papers, then hands a set to Bill, a set to the president, and keeps one for himself. I glance down at what I've been handed. It's twenty pages of notes.

The president states the obvious. They have some notes on the script. His tone is still friendly, but the adoration-of-the-script phase of this meeting is over.

I flip through the notes, trying to get a quick feel for what this rewrite is going to entail. My heart sinks. These aren't minor notes. These aren't the kind of notes that execs give when they love a script. This is an extensive rewrite. The only question is how extensive?

The development exec says, we can go in order or start with the biggest notes first, your choice.

I say, either way is fine with me.

They decide to tackle the biggest notes first and, as soon as they launch in, my question is answered. This is going to be a *very* extensive rewrite. It's an entirely new story. I want to ask them whatever happened to "we love the script," but I don't. I know what happened.

They read the script dozens of times and the freshness disappeared. They came to know the script backward and forward. They knew every plot twist before it came. They knew every character reveal before its time. Every surprise in the script became stale and they started to believe something was missing. Something here, something there, something everywhere.

In the middle of dismantling my script, the president says, you look a little disturbed.

I'm usually able to listen and respond to notes without being defensive. This is a skill that every studio writer learns. Without it, there is no career. It's easy for a writer to stand up for his vision and start a war over notes. Even a newbie can pull that off. What isn't easy is for a writer to sit through a meeting, without betraying any hint of hostility, as he watches his script getting dismantled right before his eyes.

Working writers know that producers and execs are paying for the opportunity to mold their scripts. If a writer is cashing their checks, he can't be defensive when they're exercising their rights. There may come a time when a writer has to go to war, but it can't be over the fact that the people paying him are giving him notes.

I tell the president, no, I'm not disturbed, I just like a good part of what we already have.

I leave it at that, but I want to add that the script is strong and we shouldn't be looking at a page-one rewrite.

The president says, I like a good part of what we have, too.

And then we have a familiar conversation. The conversation that takes place during every notes meeting where the writer and the execs aren't on the same page. He and his exec explain how their notes aren't really major changes and I say that I just want to make sure I understand exactly what they want.

After this conversation, we get back on track.

But as I'm listening to their notes without betraying any hint of hostility, I start to wonder if Bill was in on this ambush. Did he know in advance that these notes were coming? When the exec first handed them to me, I'd glanced at Bill. But he didn't make eye contact. His attention was focused on the president and I'd thought, that's exactly where it should be focused. But now I'm thinking he didn't make any eye contact because he knew this was coming. And, as the meeting rolls on, Bill starts to weigh in on the notes, piling on his own notes, and agreeing with the president, more and more. To me, this is proof that he was in on the ambush.

After four hours, the meeting finally winds down. I congratulate myself for making it through without showing any more hints of defensiveness. Considering how much I believe in this draft, and that this meeting was three times longer than the average notes meetings, I'm proud of myself.

The president and his exec end the meeting by reiterating how much they loved the script. Then they tell me that they're really looking forward to reading the next draft.

Bill and I walk to our cars and I wait for him to speak first. I'm curious to see if he confesses to being in on the ambush.

He doesn't. Instead, he launches into how ridiculously long the meeting was and we both agree that it was way over the top. Our conversation is strained. He knows that I expect him to say something substantive about the meeting. Like acknowledging that this a major rewrite. But we approach his car in silence.

At his car, he turns to me and says, that was a lot to absorb, but there was some good stuff in there. Why don't you spend a few days going through it and then give me a call?

I've heard this dozens of times. It's the way a producer tells a writer to remain calm. Don't do anything rash. It's a nice way to state the truth: Suck it up and find a way to make those notes work even if it's a page-one rewrite.

65

On the drive home, before calling Kerry (with Ben fired, Kerry is now my primary agent), I take a few minutes to think things through. I know Kerry is waiting to hear how the meeting went and I only have two choices. "Great" and "bad." Without a doubt, this one falls into the bad category. But I'm not sure I want to tell him that.

I could say that the meeting went "great," and then humbly retire to my cave and start the rewrite. I'd focus on the notes that might improve the script and ignore the rest. But in this case, that would mean ignoring almost every note the production company gave me.

I know that the next step is to write a better draft. That's always the next step. And in most cases, that's what the buyer expects and that'll make the buyer happy. Still, in this case, the buyer expects a completely new script.

There were times in my career when I'd stood up for a draft and fought hard for it. And there were times when I'd gone back to my cave and dove into the rewrite, even though I didn't agree with the notes. With this script, I truly believe that I have a good draft. It doesn't need an overhaul. I'd love to take what I have and make it better, not start again. The best rewrite is a rewrite that digs deeper, not a rewrite that throws the baby out with the bathwater.

As I crest Laurel Canyon, something else dawns on me. This time Kerry truly loves the script. Maybe he'd join me in standing up for it. After all, he'd turned over a new leaf. He'd said that the script was the best thing I'd ever written and, a few weeks ago, he'd also told me that he couldn't wait to show it to the town. He was sure it'd create a buzz and that Hollywood would stand up and take notice.

I log in my call to him and he takes my call right away. He asks me how the meeting went and I tell him, "okay." Honesty wins out. If I want him to protect my script, I have to tell him what's really going on. He wants to know what I mean by "okay" because he's already translated it into "bad." I explain that they want to dismantle the script and I throw out some examples.

Kerry responds by saying things like "that's not a bad idea" and "I can see that." This drives me to go into more detail. I want to make sure he understands the "ripple effect" of the changes. The "ripple effect" is how one change ripples through the script requiring numerous other changes until the whole house of cards crumbles.

Kerry says he understands the ripple effect and he seems to understand it all too well. He responds to each of the notes I throw out like he, himself, had sat in on the meeting. And, as he gives some of the major changes a ringing endorsement, I suddenly realize *why* it seems like he'd sat in on the meeting. He has a set of notes, too.

I ask him if he does and he comes clean. But not in a guilty way. He says, of course, I do, that's my job.

I park in front of my office, realizing that I'd fingered the wrong conspirator in the ambush. Bill hadn't been part of the ambush, Kerry had. He'd talked to the production company before our meeting. They had sent him their notes and they'd told him what they expected, a page-one rewrite. And from what Kerry was saying to me, it sounded like he had agreed with them.

I ask him, whatever happened to this being the best script I'd ever written? Whatever happened to showing it all over town so they'd stand up and take notice?

He says that's not exactly what he said, and he keeps repeating that it's going to *become* a great script. He's totally calm and, of course, I come across as being defensive. I *am* defensive. He could've called me in advance and told me to expect a massive set of notes, *and* he could've told the production company that the script doesn't need that much work. Instead, he chose to be part of the ambush.

I tell him that we shouldn't throw the baby out with the bathwater, but as soon as I say this, I remember who I'm talking to. The guy who always throws the baby out with the bathwater. Why am I arguing? Kerry is back to his old self. The new leaf he'd turned over was just temporary camouflage. He hasn't changed. I'm on my own.

66

The next morning, I'm in my cave and I'm concentrating on the Principles. They'll shed light on what I should do about rewriting "Buggs Lake." But no matter which way I go, the project could fall apart. If I write a completely new draft, a page-one rewrite, and it's not as strong as what we now have, the production company could easily lose interest. But if I stand up for the current draft, that could kill the project too. So with the pilot dead, I'd be left without any projects moving forward toward production.

At least, my Warner Brothers pitch is moving toward a buyer. And at least, I'd be collecting a paycheck for rewriting "Buggs Lake." Then I realize that I'm not sure about that and I email Kerry to ask him if the production company is counting this as the official second draft. Within a few minutes, he emails me back, "you're getting paid."

I know that's a good thing, but I feel like the tide is turning. And the weirdest part is that I don't feel too badly about it. I'm going to continue to implement the Principles even if I have doubts about what came first in my notebooks, the fall or abandoning the Principles.

And for some reason, this time I don't sweep those doubts under the carpet. I let myself dwell on them and I'm suddenly struck by a simple truth.

Doubt leads to change and change is exactly what I'm feeling. Falling off this wave doesn't feel like falling off that wave from long ago. I'm not as disappointed. My reaction has changed. *I've changed.*

I look at my Principles and I wonder if I'm missing a Principle. The Principle of Change. It's nowhere on my list. I do remember that some self-help books mention it. I also remember coming across it when I'd dug into the Western canon. Heraclitus, a Pre-Socratic Greek philosopher, believed that the only constant was change. He'd said that everything flows and nothing stands still. Why hadn't this Principle made it into my notebooks?

I know why. I hadn't deemed it to be one of the keys to success.

I start to wonder if this Principle means that all of my Principles are subject to change? The Principles are odes to permanence. They're commandments set in stone. Or is it possible that's not right? Maybe they're commandments, but they're *not* set in stone. Maybe the commandments change. Maybe they change when they're related to my life and not my career?

That could be it. They're down-and-dirty keys to success, but by digging deeper, they change into Principles about life.

This leads me back to luck. Luck is another term for randomness and randomness is the greatest form of change. Unexpected and unpredictable change. And sometimes devastating change. Like death.

But death, itself, *doesn't* change. Death *is* permanent. Death *is* set in stone. I haven't found a sign that shows me otherwise.

I will remember in my heart,
How we skipped and jumped
And played together.
I will love you forever
But now I must go.

Is death the exception to change? *Now I must go.* Forever. Is death where this Principle proves false? That would explain why I live in a deadworld and why I have a hole in my heart. Death is the one thing that can never change.

Then, out of nowhere, I get an epiphany. *What if death is the greatest change of all?* Both for the person who dies, innocent Sarah, and for the person who loved her, me.

In the sky there is a spirit that created us,
Poor and rich,
High and low,
Sick and well,
Mean and nice.
These are the people He put in our world.

We will always be here,
Even after we are gone.

We will always be here. But not like you were before, Sarah, is that what you mean? You will always be here, but now you've changed.

I can't believe that the heartbreaking sadness of death is the greatest example of the Principle of Change. That makes death into some kind of positive example. It has to be that death is the harsh exception to this Principle. Death is final. Permanent. There is no change at all.

I have to admit I'm not sure. *We will always be here, even after we are gone.* I'm sure about one thing. Death changes everything. Not just for the dead, but for the living. It kills them, too.

67

For the next few days, I continue to implement the Principles and I write. I work on moving my other projects forward and I let Don't Know, Don't Go, work its magic on the page-one rewrite decision.

Then I get an email from the president of the production company. He wants to know if I have any questions about the notes, now that I've had some time to think about them.

Yeah, I have some questions. Why can't you go with your original gut feeling about the script? You loved it, remember? Why can't I work on that draft?

I don't ask him any of these questions. Instead, I compose a friendly reply telling him I'm about to dive into the rewrite and I don't have any questions yet. I hit "send" and I realize that Don't Know, Don't Go, has worked its magic. I'm going to do the rewrite.

I'm fairly sure that my decision stems from the feeling that it's more important to figure out what's missing from my writing and my life, than standing up for this draft. Especially because I know that I'm close to discovering the answer. I'm also fairly certain that the answer is going to help me climb out of my deadworld.

I work diligently on the rewrite and I start to believe that I can write another great draft. I want the production company and Bill and even Kerry to love this draft as much as they loved the original draft. I want to love it, too. I also want the production company to move forward into production with this new draft.

Meanwhile, the Warner Brothers' pitch gets moved a few times. But that's okay. I'm used to it. In Hollywood, meetings get moved more times than there are days in a month. No one is committed to any meeting. If a better meeting comes along and it conflicts with a weaker meeting that's been on the books for weeks or even months, the weaker meeting gets reschedule. That's standard operating procedure.

I'm immersed in the rewrite and I'm also moving my other projects up and down my list as dictated by the Principles, and working on those projects accordingly.

I still feel like I'm falling off the wave, but I've noticed something new. When I focus on the Principles, I think about how they apply to my life and my writing. They're not just down-and-dirty keys to success. I think about them in relation to climbing out of my deadworld.

68

Rachel has added more days to her job. She loves her job and whether she's happy or not, she's happier. I know she still has a hole in her heart. She tells me. And she still cries when we talk about Sarah. But my reaction to her tears has changed. I don't avoid talking about Sarah as much as I did. Instead, I find myself telling stories about Sarah as Rachel cries and smiles and laughs, all at the same time.

Tonight, after Jake falls asleep, Rachel brings Sarah up. The purple wild flowers on the hill across from our house are blooming. Sarah loved those flowers. Every spring, she'd pick a few and give purple bouquets to her friends.

I don't change the subject. I tell Rachel a story about Sarah.

When Sarah and Jake were toddlers, we didn't expose them to the local TV news, an endless parade of murders, robberies and kidnappings. We didn't want them to think the world was a nasty, brutish place.

Then, a houseguest cracked open our protective cocoon. He liked to watch the local news every night. He'd watch it in the family room and, whenever he did, we kept Sarah and Jake away. We did a good job of it too, until the last night of his stay.

Sarah wandered into the family room to hang with him and he didn't shut the TV off. He thought we were way too protective and he didn't have a problem with Sarah catching a glimpse of the "real world."

Later that night, when I was tucking Sarah in, she told me she had something important to tell me. She looked at me like she was about to reveal a horrible secret. A secret that no one should have to bear alone. Then, in a tiny, scared voice, she told me that someone had shot someone else today and killed them. She felt so bad that it made me feel bad.

I told her as gently as I could that sometimes people do bad things. Terrible things. But just sometimes, not all the time, and this was one of those times.

She blurted out, "You mean people *still* kill people?!" Like how the hell is this possible? She explained that she thought people had stopped killing each other a long, long time ago. She thought it was something that only happened in the "olden days," when people were still savages and didn't know any better. How could it be possible that it was still happening today?

I had to confess that people still killed each other. She didn't ask why. She knew there wasn't really any good reason why, and she knew she'd have to change her view of the world. It was more brutish than she'd thought.

I finish telling this story and Rachel is smiling through her tears. The look on her face is bittersweet. But bittersweet is a hell of a lot better than bitter. It's joy and sadness mixed together, with longing thrown in. It's what I'm starting to feel when I think about Sarah.

69

I finish the rewrite of "Buggs Lake." It's good, but I don't think it's as good as that first draft. That's because the new story isn't as organic to the concept. But that doesn't matter. My job was to make the new story work as well as it possibly could and I think I did.

I give "Buggs Lake" to Kerry and, this time, he doesn't say it's the best thing I've ever written. He's back to his old self. He gives me a set of notes that speak to a completely different version of the story, not the one I handed him, but the one he'd like to see. I listen politely to his notes and then I implement the notes that improve the script and I give the draft to Bill.

Bill promptly reads it and he likes it, too. He gives me very few notes, all organic to the new story, and I can't help but think that his lack of notes is because, deep down, he knows that this draft isn't as good as the first one.

I implement his notes and I turn the script into the production company.

A few days later, I get a call from Kerry. I have no

reason to suspect that this call is about "Buggs Lake." I'm expecting to hear directly from the production company. I pick up, hoping for good news on some other project, but Kerry says that he's heard from the production company.

I know that whatever follows isn't going to be good. If they had liked the new draft, they would've called me themselves.

This kind of call, which every writer receives from his or her agent, is the opposite of an ambush. It's the softening up of the writer before the heavy bombing begins. The production company wants Kerry to prepare me before their call. They want to make sure that I don't lash out at them when they tell me that they're not happy with this draft.

So how bad is the news? Kerry tells me that the production company doesn't like the script. They want to try *another* version.

I'm thinking, of course, they don't like it. It's not as good as the first draft and that draft, the one that everyone loved, is now the gold standard in the back of their mind. I call this phenomenon "the subconscious gold standard."

A great example of the subconscious gold standard comes from a director whom I've known for many years. He boarded a studio project and before he began working with the writer on the most recent draft, he sat down and read the previous drafts. All fourteen of them.

He started with draft one and read them in order. He found that draft three was perfect. It was kink-free and the story was fully realized. He was sure that the execs at the studio had long ago forgotten about that draft, but that all the later drafts were a subconscious attempt to recreate the magic of that third draft. He was also sure that the execs had loved that draft when it first came in because that draft was *the* draft for two years, more than eight times longer than any of the other drafts.

But sometime during that draft's tenure, it started to lose its freshness. The execs knew the story so well that they started to believe something was missing. Something here, something there, something everywhere.

The next eleven drafts never recreated the magic of that third draft. It had become the subconscious gold standard.

I ask Kerry if the production company brought up the first draft of "Buggs Lake." Do they want to go back to that draft and rewrite that version of the story? He says it didn't come up and he tells me that they have some great ideas for a new take. They're sure that the new take will get us there.

I'm waiting for him to tell me that they're going to pay me for this new take since it's not a polish or "courtesy" pass, which a writer is expected to do for free. I've already completed my two steps so Kerry would have to negotiate a new deal. He doesn't volunteer this information and I finally ask him and, without hesitation, he says "no."

Then he goes on to explain that this project is their number one priority. They want to make this film. He says that I should go in there and listen to their notes before making a decision. What he's really saying is, go ahead and do the free rewrite, but take it one step at a time. His strategy is to make sure the production company knows they're getting a free rewrite, that they know I'm doing them a good deed. In today's Hollywood, that's almost all the leverage a writer has.

I've done many free rewrites over the years, so I'm not thinking "woe is me." I'm thinking here we go again. Every single writer in Hollywood faces the dilemma of free rewrites.

I'm already weighing whether it's better to spend my time on this free rewrite or work on other projects. Except for the Warner Brothers pitch, I no longer have any projects that are officially alive. I do have new projects moving forward, but right now, they're just dreams powered by the Principles.

I get off the phone with Kerry and I wonder how long it'll take him to call the production company and tell them that he's prepared the lamb for slaughter.

70

Just like every other screenwriter in Hollywood, I've had a long history with free rewrites. Free rewrites are ingrained in the Hollywood business model. Some writers have ad-hoc policies about them and some have hard and fast rules.

The Writers' Guild has never been able to come up with an answer to free rewrites. Policing free rewrites is like trying to prohibit prostitution. It's going to happen regardless of the laws against it. And that's not a knock on the Guild. I'm pro Writers' Guild. The good they've done for writers over the decades is immeasurable, from minimum payments to health care to pensions.

Free rewrites are illegal when it comes to the Writers' Guild rules. But the reality in the screenwriting jungle is different. A writer in Hollywood is asked to do free rewrites on every job and it's tough to say "no" when there are so many more reasons to say "yes" and the habit of saying "yes" starts so early, even before a screenwriter's first sale.

The majority of screenwriters in Hollywood are those trying to break into the business. They aren't in the Writers' Guild, but they're just as critical to Hollywood's business model as the writers who are in the Guild. The next generation of Guild writers always comes from their ranks.

These writers are more akin to college athletes than minor league athletes. They don't get paid and they don't get college scholarships, yet they work their butts off for the lure of a payoff down the line. They're the R & D (research and development) for a billion dollar industry and they work for free.

And everyday in Hollywood, dozens of these writers get the call they've been waiting for. A call from a legitimate producer who says he read their script and liked it. The producer liked it so much that he wants to show it to some agents. But he adds that it needs *a little more work* before he does.

The writer thinks this is his break and why shouldn't he? It *is* his break. It's his winning lottery ticket. He doesn't think twice about sitting down with the producer, getting a set of notes, then going back to his cave and writing a free draft.

He may even write a few free drafts. And why not? He's been writing for free for months or years or maybe even decades. What's a little more free work? Maybe this is "the one" that launches him to fame and fortune and I can't come up with a counter argument as to why this writer shouldn't do the free rewrite. He's not even part of the Guild yet. He's not beholden to their rules. Who would stop him and why should they? This could be the start of his screenwriting career.

It's also one of the main reasons why free rewrites

are ingrained in the Hollywood business model.

On the other side of the screenwriting universe, it's exactly the same, but for different reasons.

I was invited to be on a screenwriting panel that included among others, Joe Willie Grant, one of the most sought after writers in Hollywood, a bona fide member of that "famous" group of screenwriters. He earned millions for his production rewrites. At one point during the panel discussion, an audience member tossed us the question that comes up at every gathering of screenwriters. She wanted to know how to limit the number of free rewrites that she was being asked to do. As usual, we had no good answers.

After the panel, I talked to Joe Willie and asked him what he thought would happen if the highest profile writers, writers like himself, all decided to stop doing free rewrites. Surely, that would stop the practice.

He leaned in to me, glanced around the room to make sure no one was eavesdropping, and said, "How can I say 'no' to a free rewrite when I'm getting a million dollars a script? You think they'd ever hire me again?"

I'd never thought about it like that. I understood why new writers felt obligated to do free rewrites. They were launching their careers. And I understood why journeymen writers felt obligated. They didn't want to be branded as "hard to work with." But I'd never realized that the most powerful writers in Hollywood couldn't say "no" either. They would look like spoiled brats.

Every writer develops his or her own policy on how to handle free rewrites. When I first started out, I decided each case on an ad-hoc basis. Many factors would go into my decisions. Who was requesting the free rewrite, the exec who worked for the producer, or the producer himself? Or was it the studio? And how extensive were the notes? And would they make the script better? And how many free rewrites had I already done? All screenwriters ask themselves these questions, plus a dozen more.

During this period, at a barbecue in Bel Air, I was chatting with Marvin Kelly, a screenwriter with a half a dozen credits to his name and a career twice as long a mine. A newbie writer joined our conversation and soon told us about his current dilemma. He was having a hard time deciding whether to do another free rewrite on a script where he'd already done two free rewrites. Two free rewrites is usually the limit for a majority of writers.

I didn't volunteer my opinion. I first wanted to hear what Marvin Kelly was going to say. Would he lead this writer through the series of questions a writer usually asks himself before making his decision?

Marvin told the newbie writer that his policy on free rewrites was to do them. *Always.* I was shocked. I'd never heard of such a policy. And I blurted that out.

Marvin explained that he didn't like to waste time debating whether or not to do a free rewrite. Why spend even one minute thinking about it? Just do it. His policy was to continue to rewrite a script, if asked, regardless of the number of drafts he was paid to write. In other words, he'd decided that he'd never be a roadblock on his own films.

That conversation had a profound effect on me. I thought, hell, why not try that policy? After all, Marvin had a long list of credits. Maybe I'd get one of my films greenlit. So right after that conversation, I decided to do free rewrites. Always.

My agent at the time didn't like my new policy. He liked the ad-hoc, case-by-case policy, which was the traditional policy on rewrites. That policy gives agents a say in the process. It also gives them a way to curry favor with producers and studios. The agents are the ones who are able to talk their clients into doing another free rewrite. They're the heroes.

A couple of years after I'd implemented this new policy, and before I could really gauge the results, I met Sam Bennett at a small cocktail party in the hills of Sherman Oaks. All the guests were on a large deck facing a magnificent orange and pink L.A. sunset. A glorious sunset that matched Sam Bennett's career. He'd written two films that were Hollywood classics. Films that had inspired me to become a screenwriter in the first place.

I was complementing him on those films, and he was looking embarrassed at the adulation, so he changed the subject. He asked me what I was working on and I filled him in on my current project, a psychological thriller in the vein of "Rosemary's Baby." He was intrigued and wanted to know more. I went into the various incarnations of the story, mentioning that I was doing a fourth free rewrite.

I guess I brought up the four free rewrites because I secretly wanted to know this esteemed writers' take on this. And when he didn't react at all, that made me even more curious, so I launched into my policy about rewrites. Do them. Always. No worrying or struggling about whether to do them or not.

Sam Bennett stared at me like I'd just admitted that I was a serial killer. Then he asked, "How'd you come up with that policy?"

I told him that I thought it might get my films greenlit. He said that it wasn't going to work.

I argued my case. I explained that I'd written a good number of studio films and I'd never had any of them produced. Maybe this would work.

He chuckled. Not in a mean way, but in a knowing way. Like it was all random and doing free rewrites wasn't going to help. After he stopped chuckling, he told me his policy on free rewrites. He never did them. *Never.*

After this conversation, I could've, and maybe I should've, changed my policy. But I didn't. I wanted to give my new policy enough time to prove itself or fail. And I knew that I couldn't be the no-free-rewrite guy. I'd seen that policy torpedo the career of other screenwriters and I was sure it'd torpedo my career too.

I gave the *always* rewrite policy a few more years before I finally gave up on it. In the end, I did years of free rewrites that didn't get any of my films into production. I did move two films closer to production than I ever had before, but I can't say for sure that it was because of this policy.

I can say that I served up free entertainment to producers, executives, directors, actors and studios at an unprecedented rate. But none of that free entertainment made it to the screen.

I'm back to the traditional, ad-hoc, case-by-case policy, but I'm always tempted to implement Sam Bennett's policy.

71

It doesn't take long for me to hear from the production company. The next afternoon, after my writing session, I turn on my phone and find that they've left a message.

I call them back and the president and his exec get on the line together. They start out by telling me how much they like the new draft. Then they segue into, "but something still doesn't work."

I could've told them that *before* I wrote one word of this version. I tried to tell them that, without being defensive, in our marathon, four-hour meeting.

They start to go through their notes and I listen. They lay out their notes like army generals laying out battle plans. Generals who don't want any feedback from the troops. We don't discuss their notes, though every once in while they ask if I understand and I say "yes" as in "yes, sir." Their notes add up to another page-one rewrite. The third one and a free one.

They wrap up the call with a promise to email me a written set of notes and they tell me to give them a call after I've had some time to absorb them.

I hang up and I think, when am I going to get the

message? Do I need to feel this kind of disappointment a million times?

But within a few minutes, I don't feel that disappointment. I find myself thinking about my writing, my life, and the Principles. I realize I should be evaluating the results of my actions as they apply to my writing and my life, not just to my list of projects.

I need to adjust my course. I need to adjust my goals. I need to adjust my writing. I need to *change*.

The river is wavy.
The boats are crowded.
The subways are packed,
The road is flooded.

My house has no roof,
The windows are cracked.
I will love you forever,
But now I must go.
I will remember in my heart,
How we skipped and jumped
And played together.
I will love you forever
But now I must go.

Now *I* must go. My old self must go. And he should take his old ways of writing with him.

This epiphany makes me happy. So happy that I focus back on the question at hand without any disappointment. Should I do this free page-one rewrite? If I don't, this project is officially dead. That's clear. That would leave me with just the Warner Brothers pitch moving forward.

72

On the day of the Warner Brothers pitch, I'm not feeling as excited as I normally would. Usually, I feel euphoric before a pitch. I can't wait to get into the room and pitch my story. And the bigger the stage, the more I'm on top of my game and that adds to my excitement.

I have a perfect record when it comes to pitching directly to a buyer. I don't mean that I've sold every pitch that I've pitched to a studio. I mean that every time I've made it into room where I'm in front of one of those few people in Hollywood who can say "yes," they've always said "yes."

The Warner Brothers pitch is at that level, so I should be feeling that sense of euphoria. But I'm not.

I rehearse the pitch one final time in the Warner's Brothers parking lot. But I still don't have that feeling of euphoria.

I meet up with the director, the producer, and their development execs in the waiting area and we banter. This part feels normal. I'm relaxed and so are they.

After fifteen minutes, we're lead into a conference

room where three Warner Brothers executives are waiting. They're all smiling, including the senior exec who can say "yes."

This is a big stage. Three high-profile studio executives, an A-level director and producer, and their development execs, all sitting in an opulent conference room, in the very heart of the coconut. I know this is a sale. It's always been a "yes." But during the small talk, I'm still not feeling that euphoria. Maybe it'll get here before I pitch.

The small talk lasts about ten minutes and then I'm up to bat.

I pitch my story. I do a good job, but not a great job. I'm surprised. I expected my pitch to be great even though I knew something wasn't right. I thought the euphoria would still somehow take over.

I leave the heart of the coconut and I'm confused.

I go back to my office and I take stock. This could still be a sale. The producer and director told me that they'd thought the pitch went extremely well. They thought my performance was great and they're optimistic.

I try to convince myself that this sale will happen and that my big-stage record will stay intact. This sale will turn my downward momentum around.

73

The next day, I get the word. Warner Brothers passed. Then a few days later, I get another dose of bad news. The producer and director attached to this pitch don't want to go out to any other buyers. This project moved up to the buyer stage faster than any of my other projects and now it's been abandoned faster than any project. Easy come, easy go.

A producer usually takes a pitch to a number of buyers, anywhere from three to eight. But the more well known and powerful a producer is, the faster he or she jumps ship after rejection. A well-known producer doesn't want his reputation sullied by collecting "no's" all over town.

When I first experienced this, I couldn't integrate it into Edward Vanvich's dictum that you had to collect nine hundred ninety-nine "no's" for every one "yes." What were these producers doing, abandoning ship so quickly? These were the top producers in town, they knew what they were doing, so what was their strategy?

Later, as I worked with more producers, I realized

what their strategy was. Producers collect their nine hundred ninety-nine "no's" over a myriad of projects, not just over a few projects like writers do. And the more powerful a producer is, the more projects he controls, so the faster he can abandon a project that's trending badly and move on to another project.

Still, I never had a producer jump ship after one pass so I'm disappointed at the sudden reversal. But the disappointment disappears as fast as it arrived and this time I understand why my disappointment is no big deal. Because of change. The change to myself, to my writing, and to my life. I'm climbing out of my deadworld.

I decide to do the free draft of "Buggs Lake" even though it's the third page-one rewrite. Making this decision isn't hard. I know that regardless of whatever change is coming, I'll still be writing. And if I'm writing, I might as well work on a project that still has a chance to move forward and this is the one project left that's still actively set-up.

I call the president of the production company and tell him that I've looked at their notes and I'm going to launch into the rewrite. He's pleased. Bill Goode, the producer, is also pleased, as is Kerry.

I get down to work and during my breaks, I think about the Principles. They created this new run in my career. They lifted me out of this new rough patch. And now they're doing their best to help me find what's missing. Even though I'm falling off the wave, it all feels right.

I think about my writing, itself. I've come to enjoy it more, but still not like in the past. I'm not feeling that drive to write as strongly, but I'm beginning to understand why. My drive to write was tied to my drive for success. And that drive was like a booster rocket. It powered my career out into space. And once my career was launched and had some success, that booster rocket fell off. But it needed to be replaced by some other force, so my career wouldn't crash and burn.

I think about this analogy a little more. Once a spaceship makes it to space, it has forward momentum. And according to the laws of physics, it keeps going unless it's stopped by another force. It doesn't need to replace its booster rocket. It doesn't need more power.

Does this mean that I don't need that drive anymore? I don't need the drive for success anymore?

Then I realize that the spaceship does need more power. It says so right there in the Principles. TAERR. Take action, evaluate results, repeat. Repeat means taking more action, and more action means more power. I need power to adjust my course.

So where does *that* power come from? Does it also come from the power provided by my drive for success? Not if my goals have changed. Not if *I've* changed.

74

I devote my time to the rewrite. I should also spend some time on my other projects. I need to move them out of my cave and into the outside world, where they have the potential to generate income. But I don't spend time on them, so I finish the new draft fairly quickly.

I turn it into Bill and he likes it and gives me a few notes. Kerry also like the draft, but he knows it's a freebie, so he doesn't pile on with his usual set of notes about the story he'd like to see.

I spend a few days implementing Bill's notes and then I give the draft to the production company. Afterward, I focus on getting some of my other projects out into the marketplace.

A week later, I get a call from the president of the production company and his exec. I expect that it's good news or they would've had Kerry soften me up again. The conversation starts out well. They like the draft and they thank me for all the work that I've done. Then they launch into the specific things that they liked about the new draft. After a few minutes of listing the good points, they start slipping in the things that still don't work for them.

I offer solutions and I also remind them that this draft is basically a first draft. It was a page-one rewrite. Now it's time to dig deeper into the story to make it great.

But they counter my solutions with radical changes and I realize that, even after I've written three completely different drafts, they want to keep throwing the baby out with the bathwater. They don't want to work on making one draft great. They don't buy the concept of digging deeper.

So I stop offering solutions and I let them get on with the rest of their notes, waiting for the other shoe to drop. The other shoe being another free page-one rewrite.

But the other shoe doesn't drop. They wrap up the call and thank me again for the work I've done. I wonder what's up?

A few hours later, I find out what's up. Kerry calls me and tells me that they don't want to continue to develop the project. The project is dead.

I absorb the blow with very little disappointment and I ask Kerry if he'd expose the original draft to an actor or director. I remind him that he loved that original draft. It's the best thing I'd ever written, remember? If we can find A-level talent who agrees, the production company will instantly change their opinion about that draft. It'll rise from the garbage dumpster of development as if it were the most beautiful Phoenix the production company had ever seen.

Kerry says he won't show the original draft around town. He has a dozen reasons why he won't and when he starts listing them, I tune out rather than get angry. He reminds me of Ben, my former agent, whose new business strategy was to say "no" as often as possible.

All the projects that I'd set-up in my climb out of my rough patch are officially dead.

75

The next day, I get to my office and I start my morning routine. I focus on the Principles. With all my living projects now dead, I'm counting on the Principles to point out which projects I should focus on next. But this morning, the Principles apply themselves to what's missing in my writing and in my life.

I think about change. I think about randomness. I think about Sarah. I think about my old self and the new self who's trying to assert himself.

I start to work on a project that has Energy surrounding it. Both internal and external Energy. I have passion for this project and it has two producers interested. I begin writing, but after an hour, I get that feeling again. My writing isn't flowing the way it did before. So I decide to work on the next project on the list. After another hour, the writing on this project doesn't feel right either.

I look over my list again and I pick out another project and start on it. This time, I stop after thirty minutes. It's not working. Writing isn't working. It doesn't feel the same. During my entire climb out of my rough patch, I never did find that flow again.

I look at my list of projects again, wondering if I should start on another project when, out of nowhere, I get an idea.

Why don't I just write?

Without hesitating, I open up a new document on my computer. A blank page. Usually, when I open up a blank page, I already know what story I'm going to work on. I know what I'm writing about. But not this time.

I stare at the blank page for a few seconds, wondering what to write about, and then I stop wondering and start writing.

I write about Sarah. I write about the Principles. I write about my career. I write about my life. Stories pour out of me. All kinds of stories. But these stories aren't the ones that usually pour out of me. These stories come from my heart and not my head. They come from that feeling that something is missing. *These stories are what's missing.*

I can't believe what I'm feeling. Euphoria. I forgot what it felt like. The feeling comes and goes as I continue to write. I can only describe it as the perfect version of flow. But even that description doesn't do it justice. It's the kind of pure Energy that's so powerful it seems to spring directly from the Energy generated by the original Big Bang. It's the force that replaces the drive for success.

I write for four hours before I lean back.

76

Over the next few days, I implement the Principles and I write. I'm not sure what I'm writing. It's made up of small stories. In the screenwriting language of Hollywood, the only story language I know, this is called "episodic" writing. That means that a script is a series of stories that may feature the same characters, but the stories don't fit so neatly into one overarching tale.

That's weird. I don't write that way. I never have. It's not the way a screenwriter writes if he or she wants to make a living in Hollywood. Ninety-nine percent of working writers make sure that every scene and every story in their screenplay relates to their overall tale. This way of writing is part of working within the Hollywood system.

But I continue to write in this new strange way, and then I get some fortuitous reinforcement that it's okay to write like this. I come across an on-line interview with Tony Gold, a screenwriter whose career spans fifty years. He's written more than twenty films, many of which are classics, and two of which are considered among the greatest films of all time.

In the interview, Gold says that he writes pages and pages and pages until he finds some life in his writing. And once he finds that life, he focuses on that part of the story. I latch onto this as if Tony Gold is personally giving me this advice at the very moment when I need it.

77

At home, we're back to being a family of four, but one of us isn't here and she won't be coming back. I love Sarah and every day I try to find joy in that and not sadness. It's getting better. But I can't say that I've found a way to turn tragedy into joy. I still think it only works one way, but I'm hoping that I'm wrong.

Over dinner, Rachel tells me that Jake wrote an essay about Sarah for school. His assignment was to write about something important that he did. Jake won't talk about the essay and he gets mad at Rachel for bringing it up. He doesn't want either of us to read it.

After Jake goes to bed, I decide to read it anyway. I'm always curious to know what he's thinking about Sarah. I turn on the computer and I find the essay. It's called "When Sharing is a Matter of Life or Death." It's about giving his bone marrow to Sarah. I'm face to face with one of my worst fears. Jake is going to lay out why he feels like a failure. He doesn't understand that no one could've saved Sarah.

I read the story and I'm riveted to it. He remembers far more than I'd thought. He describes how I agonized over the decision to let him be the donor. He remembers that there was another donor who would've been acceptable but wasn't a perfect match.

I continue to read and I find something that he'd never told me. He writes that it was *lucky* that Sarah had a twin. It was *lucky* that he was a perfect match. Of course, he should be the donor. Why was Dad so worried? The operation wasn't life threatening. The threat was to Sarah's life, not his. She's the one who'd been suffering and, if he could save her, that would be the best thing he'd ever do in his life. It was his bone marrow to give, not Dad's.

He then describes the day of the operation. He says he was scared going in, but he knew that it was the right thing to do. This was the reason Sarah had a twin brother. He says that his fear didn't compare to what Sarah had already gone through and to what she still had to go through. Three months in isolation, undergoing horrible treatments, with no friends around.

He then says that the operation was painless and that his fear was gone as soon as he recovered from the anesthesia. I'm waiting for him to get to the part where he feels like a failure. Where Sarah dies.

I'm on the last page. He says that sharing what's most precious in your life is the best thing you can do with your life. He says that by giving his bone marrow to Sarah, he gave her *one more year of life*. He'll never forget that. He says it was *the greatest thing he's ever done*.

Tears come to my eyes. He doesn't think he's a failure. He thinks he's a hero. And he's right. He gave his sister one more year of life.

78

I keep writing and the stories start to bond with each other. For weeks, I write like a man possessed and I see that my writing has changed. My life has changed.

My writing is no longer about invention. It's about discovery. I've gone from a being a creator to being an explorer. I write to uncover a story, not to invent one. Like an archaeologist, I scour the countryside until I discover a bit of a story protruding from the earth. Then I set up camp around that bit and I carefully dig out the rest, digging deep into life.

I don't feel like I'm entering another rough patch. I feel like I'm climbing out of my deadworld into my new life.

I will remember in my heart,
How we skipped and jumped
And played together.
I will love you forever
But now I must go.

My old self is going and my new self is here. The meanings of the Principles are changing and I'm not sure what they're going to reveal. But I'm sure about this: Tragedy and joy are here to stay. Change is here to stay.

www.ingramcontent.com/pod-product-compliance
Lightning Source LLC
Chambersburg PA
CBHW020559180626
46810CB00007B/2576